Frantic
(Book 4 of the Detective Ryan Series)
By Andrew Hess

Phoenix Entertainment and Development (2017)

D1523271

Acknowledgements

I always start by thanking my wife. She is my rock and she is incredibly supportive of my writing career.

Thank you to Trident Book Promotions for helping to create the teasers and the cover for this amazing book.

Thank you to the amazing readers/fans of the Ali Ryan series. You are what motivated me to continue this series.

I also had the pleasure of working with some amazing models and friends. I owe you all a big thank you for helping to bring the characters to life. (Alicia, Clinton, Eric, Karina, and Luisa)

And a special thank you to the Mayor of Lindenhurst, Michael Lavorata, for helping us with our photo shoot.

Table of Contentst

Chapter 1
Chapter 2
Chapter 3
Chapter 4
Chapter 5
Chapter 6
Chapter 7
Chapter 8
Chapter 9
Chapter 10
Chapter 11
Chapter 12
Chapter 13
Chapter 14
Chapter 15
Chapter 16
Chapter 17
Chapter 18
Chapter 19
Chapter 20
Chapter 21
Chapter 22
Chapter 23
Chapter 24
Chapter 25
Chapter 26
Chapter 27
Chapter 28
Chapter 29
Chapter 30
Epilogue
About the Author
Links
Additional books

Chapter 1-HT

Calls had been made more than a week in advance. There was fear in the air around the complex that the cops were gaining ground on their investigation into the disappearance of two local girls. Something drastic had to be done to throw the cops off the trail. It was the only way to ship out the last batch of girls to their new owners.

Two men had kept an eye on their target for the last couple of weeks. They followed her every time she left the house, every time she left class, and every time she snuck away to meet up with a guy. The men had ample opportunity to snatch their target any time they wanted. She frequented house and frat parties off-campus. It would be too easy to grab her once she was drunk, but that would let the police know their operation was a lot closer than they wanted them to believe.

The men followed her close enough to know she was planning a vacation, and planned an identical itinerary, down to the hour and a half layover on the return flight from California. The girl had visited friends that lived in San Diego, and stayed at their place for a week.

The call came in the morning of the return flight. "Javier," the man said coldly through the phone. "Is everything set?"

"Yeah, boss. I'm watching the girl get in the cab now. The flight leaves in three hours."

"Good. I'll have Dimitri waiting for you at the airport. Make sure the target doesn't get away."

"Don't worry, boss. I got this."

He followed the taxi to the terminal, but lost them when he had to return his car rental. Not having eyes on the target made him nervous. Anything could happen in the time it took him to return to the airport, get through security, and re-locate the woman. It was a risk he was forced to take.

He spent an hour making his way to the boarding gate. His eyes skimmed through each shop and restaurant until he found the woman he was searching for. Her long dark hair caught his eye as he walked into a Starbucks. She stood there in her tight blue jeans and low cut black t-shirt ordering her caramel macchiato. He stood three patrons behind her, waiting to tell the barista what he wanted.

"Can I help you?" the girl behind the counter asked.

He stared at her, his eyes scanning her body and judging if she was worth it. If it were a different time, he would've considered taking her somewhere private. But he had his orders and knew how important the target was to the boss.

"I'll take a medium coffee with milk and two sugars." The barista gave him a dirty look for not ordering it as a grande coffee.

Javier never took his eyes off the target while he waited to pick up his order. She was too busy with her phone to notice how close he was getting. He walked around the woman, inhaling the strawberry scent from her hair as he picked up his drink. He reached for his cell and snapped a quick picture of the girl. He texted the photo to his partner in New York who was waiting to intercept.

He followed the woman back to the gate just in time for the employees to call the first wave of guests to board the plane. Javier waited for his group of numbers to be called and watched his target lineup with the second set of patrons. The boss made sure he had everything he needed to follow the target, but didn't know what her seat number was. If they were far from each other, it would be difficult to get close when the plane landed. Lucky for him, all he had was a carry-on bag he planned on keeping under his chair.

Once it was his turn to board the plane, he hurried down the ramp and searched for the woman he was supposed to keep an eye on. His eyes swept from one side to the other as he moved down the aisle. Thankfully, his seat was only three rows behind hers. He would need to act fast once the plane landed to get through the crowd before too many jumped in front of him.

He rested for the duration of the flight. The boss wouldn't have approved since Javier was ordered to keep the target in his sights at all times. But a five and a half hour flight was too long to be staring at the back of a chair pretending not to watch another person.

Once the plane landed, Javier grabbed his bag and rushed to the line of passengers taking their luggage from the overhead storage bins. He followed the woman off the plane, staying two people behind her until they were in the airport. He called his partner the moment he broke from the pack of passengers.

"The target is on the move," Javier said.

"I got eyes on her. She's talking to someone on the phone," Dimitri replied. "She's heading inside a bar."

"I see her. What's the plan?"

"Go in and buy her a drink."

Javier hung up and entered the airport bar. He saw the target sitting at the bar trying to get the bartender's attention. He stood next to her and tried to signal someone for a drink.

"Damn, is it always this hard to get a beer around here?" The girl let out a smile, which gave Javier his opening. He signaled the bartender again who held up a finger to signal he would be there in a minute.

"What'll it be?"

"I'll have a Corona and whatever the beautiful woman would like."

She blushed. "Can I get a cranberry and vodka?"

Javier took out a twenty and slapped it down on the bar. "Keep the change." He grabbed his beer and took a long sip. He glanced at the woman standing next to him and saluted her with his drink. "I'm Javier."

"Valentina, and you didn't have to pay for me."

"I know, but I wanted to. So…are you here for business or pleasure?"

"Neither, I live here."

"Really? What part of New York?"

Valentina chugged her drink. "Look, I appreciate the drink, but I don't know you. I really don't feel like telling my business to some guy I met in an airport bar." She placed the glass on the counter and walked out.

Javier pulled out his cell and made the call to Dimitri. "She's heading your way. We need to move on her before we miss our chance."

"I'm on it."

Javier hurried after Valentina. He could see a man dressed in black closely following their target. He caught up to them as Dimitri pressed something against the small of her back.

"Don't make a sound," he whispered into her ear. Just do as we say and you won't get hurt."

The two men rushed Valentina out of the airport and shoved her inside a white van. They joined her in the back as the driver hit the gas.

"What do you want?" she asked.

Dimitri dialed a number on his phone, which went to voicemail. "You fucked with the wrong people, Lieutenant Esposito. Now your daughter will pay for the business you cost us." He grabbed Valentina by the hair.

She screeched into the phone, "Daddy!"

The call ended with Dimitri smiling at the girl. "Time to take you to your new home."

Chapter 2-Ali

How can things change so drastically in such a short period of time? One moment I was on top of the world, and the next I'm thrown into complete chaos. I guess that's something I should be used to by now. I just finished my third high profile case in a row. Unfortunately, all of them had been orchestrated by a man who wanted me dead. He violated my privacy; he attacked me, and killed my boyfriend. I figured my life would quiet down now that Officer Reyes, AKA the Puppet Master, had been arrested. I shot and killed his partner, Dr. Claire Cain. Typical protocol would have placed me on the bench until an investigation determined it was a clean shoot. Instead, I was racing from Poughkeepsie down to JFK airport.

"Are you sure it was her?" I asked as Lieutenant Esposito sat in the passenger seat muttering curses under his breath as traffic slowed us down. "Lieu, are you sure it was her?"

"I think I'd know my own daughter's voice." He slammed his hand on the dashboard. "Stupid fucking traffic; where's the damn lights and sirens on this car?"

"It's my personal vehicle."

"Well, we should've taken a squad car."

"It wouldn't survive my driving." I cut-off a driver and then another, forcing my way in front of everyone, barely missing the front bumpers several times. Usually the lieutenant would be complaining about my driving, but when his daughter's safety was at stake, he was glad I was behind the wheel.

I could see another car mimicking my moves, but was failing to keep up. It didn't make sense for four people to pile into one car. James and Rodney decided to travel together. Rodney said it would give him a chance to get to know James a little more. But we both knew the truth; he couldn't handle my driving. James, on the other hand, could match me every step of the way. He probably would've been right behind me had another driver decided not to speed up to block him.

"What's the matter? You getting slow on me?" I joked at James's expense as he met us at gate four.

"Laugh it up, sweetheart. It's not my fault my girl is a more reckless driver than I am."

"Cut the kissy face crap and get inside," the lieutenant snapped. "We have a lot of work to do to find my daughter." We followed him inside and badged our way through the airport. "I need to speak to someone in charge."

Employees scrambled to get a manager over to us. "Can I help you?"

"My name is Lieutenant Esposito. A woman was kidnapped from this airport an hour and a half ago. I need access to the security footage."

The airport manager gave a quizzical look. "Can I see your badge again?" he asked. The lieutenant complied with the request. Once he was satisfied, the manager excused himself to make a call. He returned moments later. "I'm sorry, lieutenant. Do you have a warrant?"

"We didn't exactly have time to stop at the courthouse on our way over here. The kidnappers have a nearly two hour head-start on us."

"I'm sorry; it's policy. I'm unauthorized to allow you or anyone to view or take the security footage from the airport without a warrant." The manager walked back to his office leaving the lieutenant and I standing there in shock. A woman's life was on the line and the airport manager hid behind their bullshit policies.

We returned to find Rodney and James talking with a few of the employees of nearby shops. "Did you find out anything?" the lieutenant asked.

"No," Rodney replied.

"There's too many people coming through here every day," James sighed. "It'll be nearly impossible for anyone to remember someone passing through."

"Then we need that warrant," the lieutenant spat.

"I'm on it." I grabbed my phone and dialed the only person who could possibly expedite this type of warrant. "Hi, Richard; it's Ali. I need a huge favor."

"Sure, what do you need?"

"Lieutenant Esposito's daughter was just kidnapped from JFK airport. We need to access the security feeds, but they won't let us without a warrant."

"And let me guess; you want me to get you that warrant?"

"Yes, and we need it fast."

"Ali, the airport isn't in my jurisdiction. It's not like I can whip up a warrant and have you trampling over someone else's yard."

"Then tell me who I need to talk to. We can't wait around all day for someone else to do their damn job."

"Look, I get it. You're racing the clock. Let me make some calls and see if I can get a judge to issue the warrant."

"Thank you. In the meantime, we'll try to talk to some more employees to see if they saw something." I walked back to the group and let them know I spoke to D.A. Richard Garrett.

"Thank you, Ali," the lieutenant said. "I'll make some calls of my own. Hopefully someone will help us."

"Great. James and I will keep talking to anyone who looks like they work here. Maybe someone will recognize Valentina."

"I'll start with the employees working the boarding gates," Rodney said. "You guys wanna…" Rodney trailed off as James pulled his cell from his pocket and walked off on his own. "What's up with James?"

"I don't know." I stared at him pacing around talking on the phone. He placed his cell back in his pocket. "Everything all right?"

"Yeah, it was a telemarketer."

I could tell when James lied to me. His voice gets lower and his eyes shift from side-to-side. "Okay, well we need to look for more people to question."

"Look around you," James laughed. "I don't think there's a shortage of people. But it might be hard to find someone that saw her."

"Well, we need to do something."

"Yeah, the quicker we find her, the quicker you and I can plan our vacation." I could hear his phone ringing in his pocket. James pulled it out and glanced at the name before placing it back.

"Is that all you can think about?"

"A week off from work, you and me sitting on a beach without having to give a shit about any cases is my idea of a great time. Plus, I get to see you in a bikini all week."

"Not like you would let me leave the hotel room."

"I like that idea better than mine." His phone rang again, but this time James refused to look at it."

"Do you need to take that call?"

"No, it's nothing."

"Are you sure?"

"Yeah, it's just some asshole. He can wait until we find the lieutenant's daughter."

"Well, that's not gonna happen just standing around here. I'll take these three shops and you take the other side."

As James walked away, I could hear his phone ringing again. He glanced back to see if I was watching. *Yeah, I saw you. But what the hell is going on?*

We spent over an hour asking airport employees, bartenders, and passengers if they saw Valentina. The lieutenant sent us pictures of his daughter to show around. There were a few guys that made remarks of "Damn, I wish I saw a fine piece of ass like that." Others just whistled or made grunting noises when they saw her photo. The general consensus was no one remembered seeing her.

I met back up with the group by the boarding gate Valentina had come through. "Tell me someone saw something," the lieutenant said.

We all shook our heads. It was as if Valentina disappeared the moment she got off the plane.

"I can call the D.A. and see where he is with that warrant," I chimed in. James shot me a dirty look because he knew the D.A. had a thing for me. He caught us out on a date once and basically threatened the man's life for going anywhere near me.

"No, we don't have time to sit around on the chance he can get it. We need to do something now. My daughter's life is at stake." The lieutenant shook his head while looking around the airport. "Fuck it; I'm doing something about it." He rushed towards the manager's office and knocked on the door.

"Lieutenant Esposito, how can I help you?"

"Your warrant is almost here. I need to see the security footage now. Every minute we waste gives the kidnappers more of a chance to get away."

"Come with me." He brought us to another room where there were countless monitors showing the live feed from the airport. "I'll instruct Jordan to queue up the footage for you to watch on this monitor. Once I have the warrant, you can watch the video."

The airport manager stood next to the lieutenant shielding his view of the monitors. "Ali, didn't you say the D.A. was bringing the warrant here?" the lieutenant asked.

I knew he was lying. We didn't even have confirmation we were getting the warrant. But I understood what he wanted me to do. "Let me call him and see where he is."

"Great. Detective Johnson will wait with you by the entrance for the D.A. to arrive." The manager gave a glaring look at the lieutenant, but remained in the room.

"I'll wait until I know he is close by."

The lieutenant nodded to me and I took that as my cue to exit. I retrieved my cell and dialed the D.A. "Richard, where are we with the warrant."

"I'm waiting on the judge to sign-off on it and then I'm sending it."

"We can't wait for it to be hand delivered. I need you to fax it over the moment you get the warrant."

"Ali, we're stretching the rules enough as is; we can't push this any further."

"The lieutenant is about to do something stupid. I need something that shows we have the warrant and the full physical copy is on its way."

He took a minute to decide. "Fine, but this better not blow up in your face. Give me the number."

"Thank you. I'll text the number in a minute." I walked back inside the office and searched for a fax machine. I typed the number onto my phone and sent Richard the message. I re-entered the surveillance room where Lieutenant Esposito and the airport manager continued to have a stare down.

"Do we have an ETA on the warrant?" the lieutenant asked.

Richard's words of caution replayed in my head, but I had to do whatever it took for us to watch the surveillance video.

"He just got off the Belt Parkway."

"Then he should be here in a few minutes," the lieutenant chimed in quickly. "Officer Johnson will escort you. Once you are satisfied, he can radio back to give permission to view the video."

"Fair enough." The airport manager moved towards the woman sitting in front of the monitors. "Do not let them anywhere near this until you hear from Officer Johnson or myself; is that understood?"

"Yes, sir."

He left the room with Rodney at his side. We waited in silence for someone to give the word, but of course no one was going to. The D.A. wasn't on his way. The lieutenant and I both knew it. He wanted the manager out of the way so he could hatch whatever plan he concocted in his desperate mind.

"Ali, would you mind getting me a cup of coffee?" the lieutenant asked. He knew better than to ask that kind of favor from me. I wasn't the coffee girl, and he knew what kind of hell I would unleash if I was treated as such.

"Sure, lieu." I left the room and searched for their coffee machine. I made three cups to make sure I wasn't asked to do it again. When I returned, I saw James putting the moves on the girl guarding the computer. "What the fuck?"

"Ali, calm down."

"I leave the room for a minute and you start talking to some skank."

"Excuse me?" the girl screeched. "How dare you call me a skank?" She took a few steps towards me before James pulled her back, but further away from the computer.

"You're a piece of shit." I took the cup of coffee in my right hand and threw it at them. James moved out of the way just in time. The brown liquid splashed against Jordan's clothes. I knew it wouldn't burn her. I tested the temperature before throwing the coffee.

The woman screamed and stormed out of the room. "Well, that went better than expected," the lieutenant said with a smirk. "Now let's find out what happened to my daughter before they come back."

What we were doing was illegal, but I couldn't blame the lieutenant for risking everything. He was desperate to find his daughter. I wasn't a parent, but I knew I would do the same if my sister Amanda was in danger.

We skimmed through the footage to view the boarding gate Valentina's plane arrived at. "There she is," the lieutenant said while pointing to the screen.

There was no one walking near her, and no one acted suspicious. She didn't seem like anything was off. "Follow her on the cameras," I commanded.

James messed with the controls, turning the screen black. "What did you do?" the lieutenant snapped.

"Hold on; I'll get it back up." James tweaked the controls again, turning the screen back on just in time to watch Valentina walking past several bars and shops we visited earlier. She was looking over her shoulder nervously and walked into a man wearing a black hoodie.

"Can we get a close-up on that guy?" I asked.

"Don't you touch those controls, Detective," Esposito barked. "Just watch the damn video. I need to see what happened to her."

The footage played on as we watched the man shove something into Valentina's stomach. She was spun to the man's hip as they walked side-by-side. Another man followed closely until they reached the doors.

"So, we know she was taken by two men." I moved towards the computer to find a different angle. We needed to get more of a description on the two men, and black hoodies with blue jeans wasn't going to cut it.

He's on his way back and has Port Authority with him, Rodney texted. I showed it to the lieutenant immediately.

"James, move the footage back to the starting point. Ali, get out of here, now."

"What? Why?"

"You need to trust me."

"Okay." I rushed out of the room, grabbing the paper from the fax machine, and slipped out of the office right before the Port Authority Police arrived.

They entered with purpose. I wanted to follow them, but decided to trust the lieutenant's order. I waited until Rodney showed up at my side.

"Why aren't you inside?" he asked.

"Lieu, told me to get out right after you sent the text."

"We need to get in there and make sure they're okay."

We took a few steps towards the office when the door opened. Three men escorted James and the lieutenant out.

"What's going on?" I asked while trying to act mildly surprised.

"Who the hell are you?" an officer asked.

I held up my badge. "Detective Ali Ryan, I'm with the Ulster County Police Department."

"Well, you're infringing on our jurisdiction, detective. You have no business here."

"I beg to differ. A girl was kidnapped from this airport. The D.A. sent over a search warrant for us to view the security footage." I held up the papers I took from the fax machine. Thank god Richard came through for us.

The officer took the papers and laughed. "This doesn't mean anything. You still have no right poking your nose around here. I don't believe your people cleared it with Port Authority."

I wasn't going to argue with the officer. He was right. We had no business being there. If any other girl was kidnapped from the airport, the Port Authority police would handle the investigation. We wouldn't have been notified. The only reason we were there was because the victim was the lieutenant's daughter.

"I advise you four to leave immediately, and let us handle the investigation." The officers left us to go back inside the office as if that was the final word. They apparently didn't know me at all.

"What do we do now?" Rodney asked.

"I'll be right back. I have a call to make." I walked off grabbing my cell and dialing a number of an old friend who owed me a favor. "Jim, it's Ali."

"Uh oh, what kind of trouble are you in?"

"None, why would you think that?"

"Because we haven't talked in almost two years. So that means you're either in trouble or you need a favor."

"Okay, I did call to collect. My lieutenant's daughter was abducted from JFK airport. Port Authority is here and kicking us out. I need you to get us on the case."

"Ali, that's a big favor. I don't know if that's something I can do."

"Please try. We've already wasted enough time playing games with this airport manager and jumping through hoops to get the warrant for the security footage."

"I understand. I'll see what I can do."

"Thank you." I walked back to the group and found the lieutenant red in the face. "What happened?"

"The captain just called," the lieutenant replied. "We're all ordered back to the station immediately. Let's go."

Chapter 3-HT

The drive to the complex was long. Javier and Dimitri remained silent during the journey. They never said a word to the driver. The only sounds that filled the van were Valentina's whimpers as she came face-to-face with the realization of how much trouble she was in. There were no seats, only a mattress pad the men sat on.

"You look uncomfortable, sweetheart," Javier said in a fake caring voice. "You should come…sit with us."

Valentina couldn't take sitting on the floor of the van any more. She crawled to her feet and inched closer to the mattress. Both men occupied the edges, but left a large space behind them.

"Excuse me," she said while trying to slip between the men.

Javier grabbed her hand. "Not back there, sweetheart. I got a perfect spot for you right here." He patted his lap and smiled. His grasp on her wrist tightened as he pulled her towards him.

"Fuck you," she spat while ripping her arm away. "I wouldn't sit on your lap if you were the last man on earth."

"You keep thinking that, sweetheart. We'll see how long it lasts."

The van swerved suddenly and traveled down a steep road before turning into a complex. They passed by two empty lots by the front entrance, but continued traveling down the path to the rear. There were several cars and vans parked in the back lot.

They pulled to a stop as Dimitri slid the side door open. He grabbed Valentina's hand and pulled her from the van. Her eyes scanned her surroundings, noting all of the windows were boarded up.

"Welcome to your new home, sweetheart," Javier said with a devilish grin. "Take her inside. I'll meet up with you after I check-in with the boss."

Valentina waited for the men to separate. Despite being left with the larger of the two men, she knew she stood a better chance at making a break for it when there was only one man to deal with.

"Come on; let's move." Dimitri grabbed Valentina by the scruff of her shirt and directed her towards a large building with several doors.

"Where are we? It looks like some old apartment complex."

"Where you are doesn't matter. I doubt you'll be here long."

Once Javier was no longer in sight, she decided it was time to make her move. It didn't matter where they took her. She needed to escape. Being the daughter of a cop, Valentina knew how to fight, and that's what she planned on doing.

She put on the breaks, causing Dimitri to get too close. The heel of her foot stomped on his toes, forcing him to loosen his grip. Valentina spun around, driving her knee into his groin. She was free, but knew he would recover fast. She had to do something more. She used the palm of her hand to strike his nose before slamming her fist into his jaw.

Valentina sprinted back up the path towards the entrance and rounded the corner to the steep road. She gasped for breath after the uphill run, and took a moment to breathe as she stared at the road with passing cars.

Javier appeared behind her, wrapping his arms around her body tightly. "Where do you think you're going? The party is just getting started."

"Get your fucking hands off me."

"Now is that any way to treat your new friends?"

"We're not friends."

"That's the way you want to play it, fine; let's do this the hard way."

Dimitri caught up with blood trickling out of his nose. "Sorry, she sucker punched me."

"It doesn't matter. We need to get her inside before someone from the main road sees us."

They tied her arms behind her back and carried her down the road. She fidgeted and wiggled, desperately trying to free herself from their grasp.

"Feisty," Javier said. "I like that in a woman."

"You make me sick."

"You say that now, but just wait; you'll come around soon enough."

"I doubt it."

Javier unlocked one of the doors to the large building while Dimitri held her in his massive arms.

They were surrounded by the dark hall as Valentina was brought to the back of the building. She couldn't see anything in the darkness, but kept kicking at both men until they stopped at another door.

"Put her down for a minute," Javier said as he leaned forward to unlock the door. The moment he turned his back, nails pierced his neck. Valentina had slipped her hands out of her restraints and attacked the men once again. "You fucking bitch." He curled his hand into a fist and lunged for an attack.

"Stop," Dimitri shouted as his hand blocked the attack. "The boss wants her unharmed."

He leaned in close, blowing his cigarette breath in Valentina's face as he spoke. "Fine, I'll take my revenge later."

The two men shoved her into the open space. There was little light in the room, but just enough to make out the outlines of other bodies lying on mattresses. There was an empty bed in the corner the men directed her to.

Valentina scrunched her face as she inhaled the room's scent of sex and sweat. "You can't keep me here."

"Oh but we can, sweetheart." Javier scooped Valentina into his arms and dumped her on the mattress. Her hands shot into the air scratching and clawing at anything that came near her. Javier merely laughed at her desperate attempt at survival. "Get her arms."

Dimitri grabbed both forearms and pinned them above her head while Javier snapped a pair of handcuffs around her wrists.

"You won't get away with this. My father will find me."

"Your father is the reason you're in this mess. Sleep tight, princess."

The men exited the room while listening to Valentina fight to break free from the handcuffs. The door was locked behind them, ensuring all those inside could not leave.

"Did you check-in with the boss?" Dimitri asked.

"No. I was too busy stopping our little runaway from reaching the main road. We need to update him on the mission's success. Who knows, he might let us have a piece of that fine ass." Javier glared at the door with a hungry look in his eyes.

"Get your mind off her pussy and back on business."

They exited the building and walked over to a smaller one sitting apart from the others. They entered through the glass doors and navigated their way to a heavy oak door. They knocked twice before being beckoned inside.

"Tell me you have good news," the boss said as he sat down behind the desk. "Did you complete your task?"

"The girl is locked up with the other girls," Dimitri said.

"Did she give you any trouble?"

"She's got a hell of a right hook."

"Seems like our new guest has a lot of spunk. That could be very good for business. I think we can make a lot of money off of her."

"Boss, when can we begin her training?" Javier asked with a hint of excitement in his voice.

"You're a little eager."

"I want to be the one to break this bitch."

"In due time. Right now we have to focus on moving our next shipment. The buyers are waiting."

"Boss, you sure it's wise? I mean we just kidnapped a police lieutenant's daughter," Dimitri said.

"It's even more of a reason to move the shipment. We need to move before they come knocking on our door."

"You really think they'll find us?" asked Javier.

"No, but you can never be too sure."

"What should we do in the meantime?"

"Watch over the girls for now. Once I arrange the shipment, you'll be there as security."

"What about the lieutenant's daughter?" Dimitri inquired.

"Oh, I think special arrangements will need to be made. I think she'll help draw in some bigger clients who have enough money to make us very rich."

Chapter 4-Ali

It took an hour and a half for the four of us to return to Dutchess County. There was a sense of urgency in the air. The lieutenant sat silently in the passenger seat staring out the window. But I knew what he was thinking. He wanted to get back to the station quickly so he could launch his own investigation. Normally, I would condone this, but I had no idea how he planned on working a case where the scene of the crime was nearly two hours away, and we weren't allowed anywhere near it.

We pulled into the station's parking lot, followed closely by James and Rodney. The lieutenant shoved the passenger side door open and stormed towards the building.

"You three...my office...now."

We followed him inside the station and walked to the other side to the office. "How do you wanna do this?" I asked as James shut the door behind us.

"Johnson, I want you to get an A.P.B. out on Valentina. I want all officers to work their contacts. If anyone on the streets has any information about her, I wanna know about it."

"Yes, sir." Rodney opened the door, but came to a halt as he walked into another six-foot man dressed in a police uniform. "Sorry, sir."

"Detective Johnson, is it?" The man looked around the room and nodded at each one of us. The lieutenant and I recognized him right away. The captain was notorious for his short gray hair and bushy mustache.

"Yes, sir."

"Looks like the gang's all here." He placed a hand on Rodney's shoulder. "I think you might wanna stay for the party."

The lieutenant stood up from his desk. "Captain Balor, what an unexpected surprise. How can we help you?"

"For starters, you can drop the pleasantries. There's no need to kiss my ass. I'm here on business."

"What's going on, captain?" I asked.

"I just got off the phone with my contact at the Port Authority Police. Apparently, you four have caused quite an issue today at JFK. Would you care to elaborate?"

The lieutenant stepped forward. "My daughter was abducted sometime after her flight came in today. We believe she was grabbed from the airport and decided to get a jump on the investigation."

"And you decided to act on this despite it being far from your jurisdiction, not to mention you are way too close to the victim in this case."

"I understand, but this is my daughter we're talking about."

"I know, but you can't cut through the red tape and throw out the rules just because someone in your family is in trouble."

The lieutenant started to break down. "You don't get it. Her abductors called to taunt me. They're not doing this for a ransom."

"How do you know?"

"Do I look like I have enough money to payout a ransom? This is either personal or they plan on using her to make me do something for them."

"I get it, but we still can't bend the rules. Right now, you're not a lieutenant; you are a father of a missing woman."

"Okay, he can't work the case, but what about me?" I asked.

"You, Detective Ryan, are a real piece of work. I had several little chats about you today. The first was to the D.A. after I was provided a copy of the search warrant you talked him into getting for you. Then I receive another call from the Port Authority stating they were accepting your request to work this case, but were not happy about it. Care to explain yourself?"

"You've been a cop longer than I dreamt of becoming one. You know how crucial time is with abductions. We needed to move fast, and so we did. The manager at the airport wouldn't let us view the footage without a warrant; I called the D.A. and got us one." I knew I was crossing the line. I should've bit my tongue, apologized, and took my lumps for breaking the rules. But I was outraged by the captain's unwillingness to help us. Instead, he wasted time berating us for doing our job. "As for my request to be part of the case, we need the best working on it."

The captain walked up and stared me in the eyes. "Just because you solved a few high profile cases, doesn't mean you're the best. You were lucky."

"It was more than luck."

"You're right; it was more than luck. It was a killer's obsession with you and their pride that helped you bring him and his followers to justice." One side of his lips curled into an arrogant smirk. "You almost died on multiple occasions. You need to sit this one out and take some time for yourself."

"With all due respect, sir, I need to be working on this case. I can take time for myself after we find the lieutenant's daughter."

He let out a fake laugh before taking a step back. "Well then, you'll be doing it without your team. You will report to this address tomorrow morning." He handed me a piece of paper with a number and street name scribbled across it.

"I'll go with you," James said.

"No, Detective Thornton; you will be reporting back to your station. I've spoken to Lieutenant Guinn. He said there's a case waiting for you and to report to his office first thing in the morning."

"What about Rodney?" I asked.

"I'm sure the lieutenant has other cases he needs a skilled detective on. We can't devote an entire station's resources to work a case in another jurisdiction." He looked over at Lieutenant Esposito. "You are to keep away from this investigation. Trust me; there's a lot more riding on this than your daughter's safety. I can't afford you messing it up because you can't control your emotions."

He didn't wait for the lieutenant to respond. He let us know what he had to say. He warned Rodney and the lieutenant to keep away. He forced James back to his own station, and left me to fend for myself.

I ran out after him. "Captain Balor, wait." He stopped and turned towards me. "Why don't you want any of us working this case?"

"You all have loyalty to Lieutenant Esposito. I admire that, but that loyalty can easily become a detriment to the overall case. We need everyone working it to have a clear mind and working towards the same goal."

"Then why are you letting me stay on the case when it's obvious you don't want me to be part of it? I mean; you obviously don't think I'm qualified, and you think I'm going to be too emotional."

"Detective, I don't question your ability. I think you're an asset to this station and to the force. However, recent events and cases have been personal attacks made directly at you and your family. I believe you need more time before going back out into the field to work another high profile case."

"So, then why me and not Rodney?"

"Because you have demonstrated exemplarily work with other stations. Despite your luck, your name carries some weight since you brought to justice three killers who terrorized both Ulster and Dutchess Counties. It made it easier for your friend to come through on the favor you asked of him."

"Fine, but why wait until tomorrow?"

"I told you this was part of something bigger. You'll just have to trust me on that and show up tomorrow morning where you and your new partner will be briefed."

New partner? What the hell was I getting myself into?

I returned to the lieutenant's office where he sat staring at a picture frame on his desk. I caught James and Rodney whispering to each other. It didn't matter how loud they were; he seemed to ignore everyone in the room. His eyes were glassy and bloodshot.

"It's gonna be okay, Lieu. I'll find her."

Esposito placed the picture frame back on the desk. Despite wiping his eyes, he still had the look of fierce determination. "I know you will."

"I promise; I won't stop until she's back safe and sound."

"Good. Now, unless you three have any more tricks up your sleeves or favors you can call in, I suggest you go home."

"Are you sure?" Rodney asked.

"You can stay a little longer and get the word out to the other officers. I wanna make sure we have this area canvassed in case they were staying nearby."

I doubted that the kidnappers would make the same drive we did and risk keeping their victim so close to home, but I understood what the lieutenant was asking.

"James, don't you know a few cops on Long Island."

He chuckled at my suggestion. "Yeah, I know a guy. I'll give Officer Marconi a call in a few minutes."

"Good. I know a few cops in the city I can call."

"And I'll put out the word to my old bouncer friends," Rodney interjected. "Those guys hear all the dirt on the streets."

"Good thinking," I replied. "Don't worry, Lieu, we got this."

"I know you do." The lieutenant dismissed us but asked for me to hang back for a private word. "Ali, I need you to promise me something."

"I'll bring her back alive, sir; I promise."

"Besides that; I want you to let me know when you find the guy who did this. You let me know before calling in backup or anyone else."

"Sir, that's not a good idea."

"I don't give a shit. Whoever did this took my daughter, my little girl. I don't want the son of a bitch to get a chance to beat the system."

"No, I won't let you do go down that path."

"I have no choice. These bastards took my daughter. Now, they're going to pay for it."

I didn't know what to tell him. The man had his hands tied and couldn't do a damn thing to help save his only daughter. He was desperate, and desperate men do dangerous things. There was no way I would let him put his career and freedom at risk to take the abductors down, but a part of me knew I'd do the same if I were in his shoes.

"Okay, Lieu. When I find the people responsible for this, they're all yours."

Then the lieutenant did something he'd never done before…he hugged me. "Be careful out there. You don't have us watching your back. But if you need us, all you need to do is make the call."

Chapter 5-Ali

I hung around the station for a bit, waiting for Rodney to finish rounding up the troops to hit the streets. I used the time to make a couple of calls to my contacts in Manhattan. They offered to get the word out to their fellow NYPD officers, which was a huge help. I was hopeful one of them might stumble upon a lead that could direct us to the kidnappers or the location of Valentina.

"All set, partner?" I asked as he walked back to his desk.

"Ali, you didn't have to wait for me. I could've called Mia to pick me up or taken a cab home."

"Yeah, but then we wouldn't have one last car ride together."

"No, that's okay. You've tortured me enough over the years."

"Oh stop. I promise I won't go too fast."

He placed a stack of papers in his filing bin and glanced back at me with concern. "And how fast is that?"

"I'll only go twenty miles over the speed limit."

"Sometimes I think you became a cop just so you could have an excuse for shattering the speed limits."

"You know I only do that when it comes to chasing down a lead or a suspect." Rodney gave me a look of disbelief. "What? I'm a good driver."

"Tell that to my stomach."

"Oh stop being a baby." We walked out of the station together, letting the cool evening air breeze past us. "Speaking of which, when's Mia due?"

"We got ten more weeks until the new little rugrat gets here. She swears this is the last kid."

"Is that what you want?"

"I don't know. On one hand I love being a dad. It's a great feeling, and I can't wait for the kids to grow up so I can do more with them."

"But..."

"But this job worries me sometimes. I mean, look at what's happened to you and the lieutenant. You've had a killer personally attack you multiple times including throwing you off a bridge and holding you at gunpoint. Your sister almost died at his hands, and..." I knew what Rodney wanted to say next. He wanted to bring up the death of my ex-boyfriend, Matthew. The same man Rodney spoke of killed Matthew and tried to pin the murder on him. "Now, the lieutenant's daughter was abducted."

"And now you're worried something like this might happen to your family? Rodney, I don't know who's responsible for taking Valentina or why they did it. My situation? The guy was a lunatic who was obsessed with something I did years ago. He was a psychopath. There's no way to control something or someone like that. A person like Reyes could easily be a guy on the road you crash into. He gets hurt or someone else gets hurt and they snap."

"What's your point?"

"It doesn't matter if you're a cop or not. A person like Reyes can easily snap and go after normal people like us without needing a reason. That's why he hung around that support group and targeted Dr. Cain and Nick DeFalco. He saw how fragile their minds were and exploited them for his own gain."

"Yeah, I guess you're right."

"Haven't you learned by now? I'm always right."

We both laughed while piling into the front seat of my car. I kept the drive nice and slow, to keep Rodney from sticking his head out the window from hurling.

"How are you holding up?" he asked.

"What do you mean?"

"We just put the whole Reyes thing to bed. Claire's dead; he's in jail, and you almost died."

"Oh that? I'm fine," I replied shrugging the whole thing off as if it were just another day at the park.

"Bullshit. I know you better than that."

"I'm honestly okay. Part of me wished I was able to put a bullet in his head, but I think being locked away in a maximum security prison is punishment enough."

"How long do you think he'll last once those inmates find out he's a former cop?"

"Knowing Reyes, he'll find a way to survive in there."

"What about you?"

"Oh, I would kick everyone's ass and rule the joint."

"I'm sure you would, but that's not what I meant. You gonna be okay working this case without James and me backing you up?"

"Rodney, I'm a big girl and a damn good cop. I worked plenty of cases without either one of you guys helping me."

"Yeah, but this is different."

"No it's not, but thank you for your concern. If I need backup, I'll be sure to call you guys first."

We pulled up to Rodney's house and parked in the driveway. "You know the lieutenant will be busting your ass for info every day?"

"I'm counting on it. Now go inside to your family and give them a kiss for me."

"You ever plan on settling down and working on popping out some kids? I'm sure Mia would love to set up some play dates."

"Goodnight, Rodney."

He opened the door and lingered. "I'm just saying you and James would make some cute babies together."

"We're so not having this conversation right now."

"You know I'm right," he replied while closing the door. He walked up to the house laughing while glancing back at me.

Truth be told; I only considered settling down once, and that was with Matthew. I thought about walking away from police work, or at the very least, taking some time away to marry him and one day become a mom. Since his death, I didn't think about it at all, despite living with James.

Okay, yes we would undeniably have the cutest kids ever, but we were both detectives who worked high profile cases. That wouldn't be the ideal world to raise a child in. I had been the focus of a psychopath for years, and he spent the last year and a half making my life hell. I couldn't put a kid in the middle of something like that. Hell, I tried shipping my sister back home to our parents after realizing she was a potential target and she was only eight years younger than me.

I sat in Rodney's driveway for ten minutes dwelling on those thoughts until my phone vibrated loudly in the console.

J (James): When are you coming home? I picked up a pizza.
Me: Just dropped Rodney off. On my way back now.

I pulled up to the house twenty minutes later. It looked dark inside. I looked around the block to see if any of the neighbors had their lights on or if we were in the middle of a blackout. The rest of the block appeared normal, which worried me. My gun was locked away in a safe inside the house, but I always carried a spare. I opened the trunk and removed the floor mat. I grabbed the holster and removed the gun from it before storming the front door. I turned the knob, finding it unlocked. I pushed my way inside and aimed the gun as if I was clearing a building with a potential suspect in it. As I rounded the corner to the living room, I found James sitting on the couch pouring a glass of wine next to two lit candles.

"Shit, Ali, put the damn gun down."

"Why are all the lights off?"

"I was trying to set the mood and surprise you."

I put the gun back in the holster and placed it on the mantle over the unlit fireplace. "This is the kind of surprise that'll get your head blown off."

I could see the gears in his mind turning as he thought about what I said. It was a similar setup to how Matthew was murdered; only we knew someone was coming after us. Reyes left me roses on my desk with a note suggesting he was going after my sister, Amanda. Matthew happened to be on the phone with me when I found the note. He raced to the house to save her while I hurried from the station. When I got to my place, the lights were out. We walked blindly into the house I rented and searched for any sign of Amanda or Matthew. Rodney took the back of the house while James and I searched the front. We heard a thud and a gunshot. When we raced towards the noises, we found Rodney unconscious and Matthew bleeding out.

"Ali, I'm sorry. I wasn't thinking."

"It's okay. I know you meant well." I glanced around at the coffee table to find two plates filled with slices of meatball and sausage pizza, a small plate of hot wings, and two glasses of wine set underneath two lit candlesticks. "Why are we sitting in the dark?"

He jumped up from the couch and handed me one of the glasses of wine. "I figured we both needed a night of relaxation and thought why not add some romance to it."

I grabbed the glass of wine and stared at him. "You just wanna get laid tonight."

"Damn right," he joked. "I want us to have a few drinks, forget about our jobs and all the bullshit for the night, and focus on just the two of us. If that happens to lead into another night of you being handcuffed to the bed, then so be it."

I blushed and sipped the wine nervously. "Maybe tonight is your night to be chained to the bed."

He had a far off look in his eyes while taking a gulp from his glass. "I don't think that's a good idea." He brushed off the subject and quickly walked back to the couch.

I had a feeling it had something to do with his past. Things happened so quickly between us we never really talked about anything other than our current situation. We never spoke about our past relationships. If it weren't for a random encounter where James had his friend Brad come over to help him move, I wouldn't have known James Thornton had any friends.

"Why don't we ever talk?" I asked.

"What do you mean? We talk all the time."

"Yeah, but it's always police stuff. We've never really sat down and talked. I mean, I know who you are now, but I don't know anything else about you other than you being a great cop and an amazing boyfriend."

"Don't forget how incredible I am in the bedroom."

"We can discuss your comedic performances later." He raised an eyebrow at my response. He opened his mouth to speak, but I cut him off. "Can we be serious for a minute?"

"Okay, what do you wanna talk about?"

"I wanna get to know you more."

"If you're asking to take this relationship slow, I think you're a little late for that. I mean, we're already living together."

"No, I just want to know you. Where'd you grow up? Do you have any siblings? What were you like in high school?"

He downed the glass of wine like he needed liquid courage to answer my questions. "I grew up in Queens with my mother and brother. I left home when I was eighteen and moved up here for college. I graduated with a 3.75 and stayed up here to join the academy. Years later, I met you; the end."

"I didn't know you were from Queens." Although, I should've guessed it by his accent, but I always figured he was from Brooklyn.

"Born and raised."

"Do you ever go home and visit your family?"

James grabbed his pizza and stuffed his face so he didn't have to answer. I sat there staring at him until he finally realized he didn't have another choice.

"There's nothing to go back and visit."

"Why; what happened?"

He shut his eyes and took a deep breath. "My mother passed away a few years ago. My brother and I haven't spoken since."

"What about your dad?"

"He was a marine and died overseas when I was young."

"James, I'm so sorry." I felt bad for bringing up the subject. I wanted to know more about it, but felt like I was pushing too hard.

"It's no big deal." He poured himself another glass of wine.

I decided to change the subject to something we both loved. "So, tell me about your toughest case."

"What?" he asked while a slice of pizza hung from his mouth.

"Well, you obviously know mine."

"It's not something I like to talk about."

"Why?"

"Let's just say it didn't end well. People I cared about were involved and they got hurt."

I could see my questions kept striking a nerve with James. "I'm sorry; I didn't mean to kill the mood."

"Look, I don't like talking about my past and with good reason."

"Maybe talking isn't our thing."

"I don't mind it, but I put the past behind me. I'm only concerned with present and the future." He raised his glass to his lips.

"Yeah, what do you think about?"

"Mostly you and the things I'd like to do to you. But I also think about making an honest woman out of you."

"Are you saying what I think you're saying?"

"I'm not saying I want to right away, but I could see us walking down the aisle together. What about you?"

"I-I really hadn't thought about it. I mean, maybe. I'd like to one day and possibly have kids, but-"

"So you wanna have kids? I think you'd make a great mom."

"One day...maybe."

"Then we better start practicing." He moved closer and pressed his lips firmly against mine. After the day we had, I welcomed the closeness of his body.

I heard a door slam shut. "Come on; get a room," my sister said from the entrance to the living room.

"I didn't know you'd be home tonight."

"I'm not staying. I needed to change before going to my boyfriend's house. He said he had something special planned tonight."

"If he tries anything you're not okay with, you give me a call."

"Yeah, because that'll go over well."

"What does that mean?"

"You'd try to scare him off like you always do."

I got off the couch and followed Amanda as she entered her bedroom. She rifled through her closet for a change of clothes. "I want to meet him."

"Who?"

"Your boyfriend. We should double date some time."

"Maybe. Right now, I just need to get ready." I turned to leave but she stopped me. "Look, I know this is your house, but can you not do it on the couch."

"We weren't doing anything. We were just making out."

"Yeah, we both know where just making out leads to."

"Shut up, and get ready. You don't wanna be late for your big date with Mr. tall, dark, and mysterious."

Amanda slammed the door in my face. Apparently the boyfriend teasing was only allowed when my love life was the topic of discussion.

I re-entered the living room and picked up my wine glass.

"Everything okay?" James asked.

"Just Amanda being herself again."

"I guess the night's over?"

"She's supposed to be going out with her boyfriend in a bit."

"So, she's finally going to bring him around?"

"No. She's still refusing to let me meet him."

"And I plan on keeping it that way for as long as I can," she sneered from the hall as she darted from her room. She was wearing a short black dress that barely covered her ass, and a pair of black ankle boots.

"You're going out with him looking like that?" I asked.

"He likes it when I dress like this for him."

I opened my mouth to make a witty remark, but decided it would prove Amanda's point about me harassing her boyfriends.

"Have a good time," I said with a fake smile. The door closed moments later. I grunted in anger as the headlights beamed into the house. "I hate when she gets like-" James scooped me off my feet before I could finish my sentence.

"You need to forget about your sister right now. She's a grown up and can make her own choices. The only thing you need to worry about is how much sleep am I gonna let you have tonight."

He carried me down the hall to our bedroom. He kicked the door closed behind us and sat me on the bed. James knelt on the floor, slowly unzipping my boots.

I shifted to the side and grabbed his collar. "No cuffs tonight."

"Okay." He rose to his feet and pushed me back towards the headboard. He pulled my shirt over my head. "You're so fucking beautiful." He kissed my shoulders while sliding my bra straps down my arms. "I'm so lucky to have you."

"Yeah you are."

I cupped his face with my hands drawing his attention to me. I pressed my lips against his, feeling the fire burning within. It was just as powerful as our first kiss. If he dropped to a knee and proposed at that moment, I would've said yes right on the spot. James had shown how much he's loved me ever since we met. It may have taken me some time, but I warmed up to the idea of a future with him.

The scruff of his five o'clock shadow brushed against my neck as he left a trail of kisses on my collar bone. I was surprised to find he had removed my bra without me knowing.

Damn he was good at that.

His rough fingers toyed with my pebbled nipples causing me to arch my back. I let out a groan as he kissed away the memories of the day. I lay back, letting James work his magic. His fingers tugged my jeans and panties off my hips until they were pulled from my body. I was left lying naked on the bed.

"No fair," I whined.

James stripped off his shirt letting me run my hands over his chiseled chest and the tattoos that covered his torso. There was no need for foreplay. I was ready for him, but he was insistent and was very persuasive.

I gasped as I felt his finger plunge deep within me. He smiled and seemed to revel in my reaction. He swirled his tongue around my budding nipple while using his fingers to play my clit like a violin.

Fuck I was putty in his hands.

"God, I want you right now," he groaned.

"Then fuck me already."

He wasted no time in changing positions. He inserted himself as my long legs wrapped around his waist. He rocked back and forth, letting me feel his length pushing against my G-Spot. I reached up and dragged my nails across his back, eliciting a growl from him in response.

"There's my girl."

I felt him slam into me hard, catching me off guard but loved it just the same. He picked up the pace, going harder and faster with every thrust. In minutes he had me spinning out of control. I could feel myself reaching my climax as he pinched my nipples. I dug my teeth into his shoulder to stifle my screams.

I felt his body relax as he loosened his grip on me. He rolled to my side and pulled me to his body. His muscular arms held me tight.

"This is my happy place," I sighed.

"Then I think we need to visit it more often."

"Let's hope these cases end soon so we don't have to wait long."

"About that…I really don't like the idea of you working this case without Rodney or me as your back up."

"I already had this talk with him. I'll be fine. I'm a big girl and have worked a lot of cases on my own before I met either of you."

"I know; I just don't wanna see you get hurt."

"I'll be fine." Those were my famous last words before everything goes to hell. I expected nothing less from Valentina's case.

Chapter 6-HT

Valentina sat in darkness. The minutes seemed like hours, the hours seemed like days, yet she had only spent one night in captivity. The door opened several times, but she couldn't see who entered or left the room. She didn't dare make a sound, knowing it would only bring her captors back. But she needed to find a way to escape.

She tried to slide her wrists out of the handcuffs, but they were secured too tight. It was nearly impossible for her to move since her arms were pinned above her head.

"Don't fight it sweetheart," a woman's voice said softly, cutting the silence. Valentina struggled to see where the woman was, but couldn't see anything in the dark.

"I need to get out of here."

"We all do, but there's no escape. We only get out when they let us out for their parties."

"What parties?" Valentina asked.

"Not the kind you wanna be a part of, sweetheart."

"Why? What happens at the parties?"

"You make money for these pigs."

"How?"

"Doing whatever the clients want. Use your imagination."

Footsteps echoed outside the room, quieting the women instantly. The door opened letting a sliver of light pierce through the darkness. A man entered with a woman slumped against his body. He helped her to a nearby bed and chained her to the wall.

"You did great tonight, Shaniqua," the man said. Valentina knew it was one of the men who brought her to that hell. "Rest up, we may need you tomorrow."

The woman moaned loudly as she tried to inch her way towards the man. "Anything for you."

Valentina was repulsed by the affection Shaniqua showed the man. She couldn't fathom how anyone could enjoy being near these men. Just being near them during the drive to the building made her skin crawl.

Valentina watched as the man moved towards the door. The light caught him and lit up his face. He glanced at her, causing Valentina to suck in her breath in hopes he didn't notice her watching him. He walked to the door and grabbed the handle.

He'll be gone in a minute, she thought. Closing her eyes, Valentina counted the seconds until she heard the door click shut. She let out a sigh of relief.

"You didn't think I'd leave without saying hello, princess," the man said coldly. Valentina's eyes flashed open to see him standing next to her bed. She opened her mouth to scream, but his hand quickly covered her lips. "Trust me; you really don't wanna do that, sweetheart."

The idea of the man touching her sent goosebumps up and down her body. She shook her head, trying to remove his hand.

"Calm yourself," he said in a hushed tone. Valentina complied much to the man's satisfaction. "Now, if you learn to be nice to me, I will be very nice to you." He trailed his finger along the side of Valentina's face. She grimaced against his touch, which went unnoticed.

She tried to think of a better place, somewhere she could mentally escape to while laying at the mercy of some scumbag kidnapper. She tried to picture being home with her parents, who would've pestered her for details of her trip. She would've taken that over being locked in a room with some creep.

But those thoughts couldn't block out her reality. The man kept groping her body, massaging her arms and legs as if he believed it would turn her on.

He rubbed the inside of her leg and worked his way up to her groin. She gasped as his thumb pressed against her. "Tell me something you want, anything, and I'll get it."

Valentina finally mustered the courage to speak. "If I wanted something, would you do it?"

"Sure, as long as you repay the favor."

"Okay...I know what I want."

"What's that, sweetheart?"

"I want you to eat a dick," she said while spitting at him.

"You're gonna regret that," he said with an evil grin.

"I already regret everything since I got off that plane."

"Oh just wait. You'll be begging for my mercy soon."

"I don't beg."

"You will. And I'll enjoy being the one to break you." He cupped his hand firmly on her groin and smiled.

Valentina tried to kick him, but he had already moved far enough away. "My father will find me. And when he does, you're a dead man."

"Your father is the reason you're here in the first place. You can thank dear old dad...if you ever see him again. Goodnight, sweetheart."

He took his time walking away. His lingering eyes kept glancing back at Valentina as he exited the room. She waited in stilled silence for the door to close. The moment the light extinguished, Valentina thrashed around the mattress pulling on her restraints, frantically trying to free herself before her captor returned.

Javier smiled as he exited the room. He could hear the clanking of the handcuffs hit the metal bar Valentina Esposito was shackled to. He knew there was no escape, but loved hearing her struggle to free herself. It was her fighting spirit that made her so damn attractive. It was the same fiery attitude that elicited his desire to break her.

He entered a nearby room and turned on the monitor. He could see all of the girls as they lay helplessly on their beds. Most of them were either sleeping or too messed up to know what was going on. He zoomed in on the Latina in the corner. She continued to thrash around, doing whatever it took to escape.

Javier's desires were becoming too strong. He knew he needed to wait until the boss gave him the okay to begin the process, but he didn't have much restraint left.

He continued watching Valentina until an idea emerged from his lust filled mind. He took a big gamble and dialed the boss.

"What is it?" the boss answered.

"Hey, when can we start on the new girl?"

"She's not ready yet. I'll let you know when you can begin."

"Yeah, but she's getting feisty. It won't be long until she finds a way out of those cuffs. I mean, her dad is a police lieutenant."

"And you believe this girl will pose a threat to you?"

"No, but we don't wanna underestimate her either, sir."

"Very well. You can begin phase one, but keep it in your pants for now. You are not to touch her until I give the order."

"But, sir-"

"But nothing. You heard me. If you so much as fondle her tits without my say so, I will have someone cutoff your dick and shove it down your throat. Are we clear?"

"Yes, sir," Javier said with a deflated tone.

"Good. Now, do not call me again unless it is important." The boss hung up, leaving Javier standing in the security room suppressing the urge to defy his boss.

He exited the room and went down the hall. Inside was a small room with a safe hidden behind a wall of cleaning supplies. He maneuvered himself between the two and opened the door.

Javier pulled out a black box with a syringe inside. He jabbed it into a vial that sat inside the safe, filling it just enough to give its recipient a nice long high. He returned to the security room and stared at the monitor...at Valentina.

"Let phase one commence, sweetheart."

Chapter 7-Ali

Waking in his arms every morning was the greatest feeling in the world. There's nowhere else I'd rather be. Unfortunately, I had a missing person's case to work that had the utmost importance placed on me to find the victim. I was actually surprised to see the lieutenant hadn't called me first thing in the morning, demanding an update.

I rolled to the side of the bed, but felt a pair of arms wrap around me tightly. "Where do you think you're going?" James asked.

"I need to jump in the shower and get ready. I don't wanna be late for my meeting with the Port Authority Police today."

Normally, James would've fought to keep me in the bed just a little longer. But he must've seen the determined look in my eyes, because he let go of my waist and let me climb out of bed.

"I still don't like you working this case alone," he grumbled.

"I'm sure they'll partner me up with one of their men."

"That's what I'm afraid of; how do we know we can trust them?"

James was skeptical about working with another officer. After all, I was betrayed by one of the men from my own station. I rode with Officer Reyes several times, trying to show him the ropes. Meanwhile, he plotted to kill me the whole time. I couldn't blame James for being overprotective.

"It's not like we have much of a choice. One of us needs to work this case and find the lieutenant's daughter, and you apparently have a case waiting for you on your desk."

"Yeah, don't remind me."

"Do you have any clue what it might be?"

"No, but knowing my lieutenant, it's gonna be something big and something I don't wanna any part of."

"Why do you put up with him?"

"It's complicated, but it involved a big case I worked a few months before I met you."

"Really? What happened?"

James had a distant look on his face. "Huh? Nothing. Don't you have to get ready to head back to the airport?"

Nice deflection, I thought. It was obvious he didn't want to talk about it. I wanted to respect his decision not to tell me, but planned on bringing it up again at a later time.

I exited the bedroom and walked around the house to put on the coffee pot. I peered outside while waiting for the morning brew, and noticed Amanda's car wasn't parked out front. *That's odd; she's never up this early.* I checked her room and saw the bed was still made.

"Did you hear Amanda come home last night?" I asked.

"I don't remember anything after we…" He wiggled his eyebrows suggestively. I knew what he meant and what he wanted at that moment.

"I don't think she came home," I replied while brushing him off.

"Ali, it's okay if she decides to stay over at her boyfriend's place; she's an adult."

"I'm very well aware. I just wish she would've texted me to let us know she was staying out all night." I moved towards the nightstand for my phone. "I'm gonna call and make sure she's okay."

James lunged over the side of the bed and ripped it out of my hand. "I don't think that's a good idea. You call her now, and she'll rip you a new one for calling her so early."

I knew he was right. I just didn't like that she stayed out all night without giving me a bit of a heads-up.

"Fine," I sighed. I listened to the coffee brewing as I stepped into the bathroom across the hall.

"Are you jumping in the shower?" James asked. I poked my head back inside the bedroom. "You want some company?"

"Maybe later," I replied with a raised eyebrow.

I rushed through my morning shower and grabbed a pair of black pants and blue button down. It took me fifteen minutes to get ready. It took James that long just to get out of bed and pick out his clothes. I grabbed a pair of black pumps from my closet and slipped them on as I poured coffee into a to-go cup.

It took two hours to arrive at the Port Authority Office near JFK Airport. It was a long, exhausting drive. I walked into their office, catching questioning glances with every step I took.

"Can I help you?" an officer asked.

"My name is Detective Ali Ryan. I was told to report here for the Valentina Esposito kidnapping."

The officer held up a finger and placed a call. He mumbled something into the phone and nodded his head several times before hanging up.

"Please have a seat; someone will be with you in a couple of minutes." He motioned to a group of chairs where one other person sat.

I marched over to the man dressed in dark pants and a gray dress shirt. I recognized the piece of shit occupying the chair. He was a friend of Officer Reyes. He partnered with the deceased Officer Davis. And he was also the bane of my existence.

"What the fuck are you doing here, Lombardo?" I snapped.

He looked up at me with distain. "Not that it's any of your business, Detective, but I'm here working a case."

"What do you mean?"

"Are you hard of hearing? I'm here for a case."

"What case?"

"None of your fucking business."

"It is my business if you're infringing on my case." I watched him take a breath as if he was about to respond but shut his mouth. "Did the lieutenant send you?"

There was confusion written all over his face. "He had me working a missing girl's case for weeks. I got a call last night asking me to be here today at ten."

"Who asked you to be here?"

"I'm done answering your questions. You mind telling me why you're here?"

"I'm here working Valentina's kidnapping." The whole station was put on alert. Everyone knew she was missing, but based on Lombardo's look of shock, he wasn't aware.

"I-I didn't know. How's the lieutenant?"

"He's a fucking basket case and ready to tear the whole state of New York apart trying to find his daughter."

Lombardo shook his head. "I don't blame him. I'd do the same if it was my kid missing. Let him know I'd be joining the hunt for her if I didn't have this case."

"If you're not here because of her, then why are you here? Who called you?"

"I did," a man's voice said from behind me. I turned and saw a man in his late twenties with short black hair standing there with his hands on his hips. He wore dark slacks and a white button down shirt and black tie. "Ricky, you called him?"

"Why don't you both come with me? I'll explain everything." We followed him down the hall and up the stairs.

Ricky was a friend I met while attending college. He was one of my oldest friends. We took psych courses together, and talked about joining the force. I went with local law enforcement, while he joined the port authority.

He brought us to a conference room with a long table and about fifteen chairs. "What's going on?" I asked.

"Please have a seat, Detective."

"Ricky, I think you've known me long enough to call me Ali."

Ricky's rough hands grabbed a file from the table and flipped through a few pages. "Detective Ryan, you are here to investigate the kidnapping of Valentina Esposito."

"Do we have any leads on her?"

"We'll get to the investigation in a moment."

"Then can you explain why he's here?"

"Detective Lombardo has been working multiple missing person cases; the details of which we believe are connected."

"Connected how?"

Lombardo walked around the table and grabbed the file from Ricky's hands. "The two girls we were looking into are believed to have been taken and are now part of a human trafficking ring."

"Wait…you don't think…"

"It's possible," Ricky replied. "I brought Detective Lombardo in to help with the investigation."

Oh god; please don't say what I think you're about to say.

"I believe you two will do well together. You're both great cops. Detective Lombardo can fill you in on the other two missing girls while you both investigate Valentina's kidnapping."

Ricky grabbed a remote and pointed it to the ceiling. I could hear a machine turn on as a feint light hit the wall. Ricky walked to the end of the table and opened a laptop. He clicked away on the computer until an image of Valentina appeared on the wall.

"This is the footage from the airport, the day Ms. Esposito was taken." He clicked another button and the video began.

The camera was focused on the boarding gate where a steady flow of people exited from the open door. Several minutes passed before we saw the raven haired Columbian beauty pass by toting a small bag slung over her shoulder. We watched her follow the group of people from her flight. It was the same footage we saw the day before.

She walked along the strip of bars and restaurants, only this time I saw her walk into one of them. "We need to find out the name of that bar and get their security footage."

"That'll take a warrant," Ricky replied. I returned it with a scowl to let him know I wasn't playing games. "I'll have our men check out the bar and work on getting what you need."

I heard Lombardo snicker at my demand. I didn't care what he was laughing about; I needed answers and didn't care what I had to do to get them.

Valentina sat in the bar for a few minutes before walking out. Without the footage from the bar, I had no idea what she did or who she may have spoken to while she was inside.

The video picked up outside the women's bathroom. She walked into another man who shoved something into her stomach. From the camera angle, we couldn't see what the man used to get her to follow his orders or his face. Then another man appeared next to her. The three of them walked side-by-side until they left the airport.

"They never picked up her bag," Lombardo announced.

I didn't know how that was supposed to help us, but it was a fact we needed to keep in mind. The thought didn't last long as the video cut to the trio jumping into a white van that pulled up as they walked out to the pick-up curb.

"Why didn't she try to flag security or the police down when she had a chance?" Lombardo asked.

"They probably threatened her before they walked through the doors. She had to have been scared out of her mind."

"Yeah, but there were only two men; she could've broken free or yelled to get someone's attention. The airport had to have been crawling with cops."

"That's easy for you to say, Lombardo. You're here, safe inside a room where there's no threat. She's a young woman who's being taken against her will."

"And she let it happen by not doing anything to stop them."

"Enough!" Ricky snapped. "If you plan on solving these missing person cases, you need to stop arguing and get on the same page."

He was right. No matter how much I couldn't stand Lombardo, he was my assigned partner and I needed to work with him to bring down Valentina's kidnappers.

"Agreed," I solemnly replied. I turned to Lombardo. "What can you tell me about the other missing girls?"

"So, now you're asking for my help?"

"Cut the crap. If Valentina's kidnapping has anything to do with their abductions, we need to find their connection and use it to get an ID on the men responsible."

"The first woman was reported missing three weeks ago. Her name was Katrina Gutierrez. She apparently had just returned to school after spending a week with her family in Queens."

"Who reported her missing?" I asked.

"Her roommate called it in. She told us her bus was scheduled to drop her off at the bus terminal on Main Street in New Paltz around nine o'clock and was supposed to call her when she got in."

"And let me guess, she never received the call?"

"We checked with the bus company and the driver. She rode back up to New Paltz, but they didn't know what happened to her once she got off the bus."

"Was there any evidence uncovered from her disappearance?" Ricky asked in a hopeful tone.

"No," Lombardo sighed. "We tried tracking down some of the passengers, but no one seemed to remember her or anything suspicious."

There was nothing to go on and didn't know how the first disappearance could provide any helpful information to Valentina's case. "What about the second girl?"

"Tina Marks, just graduated high school earlier this year. She was last seen at a house party on Grove Street. Her friends said she went outside for a smoke and to call her boyfriend. She never returned to the party. Her friends thought she met up with the boyfriend, but he advised us he was at home packing his bags for college. His parents corroborated his story."

"So, you mean to tell me both girls seem to be abducted, but no one saw them taken or anything suspicious. The only facts we have were they were young college aged girls taken in public environments."

"What are you thinking, Ali?" Ricky asked.

"Whoever these men are, they're good at keeping themselves hidden and are able to cover their tracks really well."

The men were good at leaving no evidence behind, but they messed up. They took the lieutenant's daughter from an airport with cameras everywhere. I didn't care how many warrants I had to secure, I would track down every bit of security footage to get one glimpse of the men who took Valentina and make them pay for it.

Chapter 8-HT

Twenty-four hours in captivity. Twenty-four hours of the forbidden fruit dangling in front of his face without having permission to do what he wanted. Javier watched Valentina from the monitor as she lay helplessly on the mattress.

His fingers drummed on the black box on the desk. It had only been twelve hours since he administered Valentina's last treatment. It wouldn't be long before she was ready for the next. He loved the fire in her eyes, but couldn't wait to break her fighting spirit. He wanted to see her cave into her own desires and accept him as her master, but it would be a while before they reached that level.

He looked at the clock and smiled. "Oh, I'm going to enjoy this."

He opened the box and pulled out a syringe. It was filled just enough to give someone a small dose of heroin. With an ear-to-ear grin, Javier entered the dark room and made his way to Valentina's bed.

"Time for your medicine," he said.

Her eyes flashed open. She tried to scream, but had a gag shoved into her open mouth. He watched as Valentina tried to fight him off, but was still bound to the bed.

"Relax, sweetheart. I'm not here to hurt you. I just wanna make you feel better." He let his finger skim along her arm. He smiled, knowing she couldn't turn away from his touch.

He freed her right arm and brought it to her side with her palm facing up. He placed the strap around her arm and lightly slapped her skin until the vein bulged. The needle danced over her arm playfully, letting Javier enjoy a few moments of toying with her.

He removed the gag from Valentina's mouth. "You'll learn to love these little visits."

"Fuck you," she spat. "I want nothing to do with you."

"Not even if I can help you escape?"

Valentina looked like she wanted to argue, but Javier's question stopped her. "What do you mean?"

"I can help you escape."

"Great. Get me out of these handcuffs and let's go."

"Not so fast," Javier said with a sinister grin. I'll help you, but you have to do something for me first."

Valentina stared at her captor in fear. "What?"

"I'll get you out of here, but first, you need to prove how bad you want out."

"What? How?"

"Let's put that pretty little mouth of yours to good use." He grabbed his crotch with one hand while cupping Valentina's chin with the other.

"Screw you."

"If you insist, but I usually like being on top."

"I wouldn't touch you if you were the last man on earth."

"You say that now, but give it some time. Trust me; you'll be begging for my cock soon enough."

"Only so I can cut it off and shove it up your ass."

He jammed the needle into her arm and pushed down on the plunger slowly. "You keep thinking that, sweetheart." He could see the fire slowly fading from her eyes. He returned her wrist to its restraint and headed out of the room. He gazed back at her one final time before exiting.

A half hour later, one of his men escorted a young brunette into the building. They had been out making money for their boss. He reached out towards the man who handed him a stack of cash.

Javier skimmed through it, counting each bill as it unfolded. "Not bad," he said. "A grand in just a few hours is pretty good for a beginner." Javier took the money and walked it back to the office leaving it in a safety deposit box inside a safe.

"You want me to put her back?" the man asked.

Javier thought about letting her go back out to make some more money, but a better idea entered his brain. "Let her rest for an hour and then take her back out." Using the back of his finger, Javier traced a line along her jaw. "This one can make us a lot of money."

He let the pair enter the room where all the women slept and waited for the man to return. "Did the boss say when the next shipment is going out?"

"No, but it won't be too much longer. I think the latest group will make us a ton of money."

"Especially that new girl. She's one fine piece of ass."

Javier grabbed the man by the shirt and pulled him close. "Keep away from that one. The boss said she's off limits."

"Damn, I was hoping to get some of that before he shipped her off."

"Until he gives the order, no one is to touch her."

Javier meant it. He gave his word to his boss she would be untouched until he gave the order. But he considered himself first in line when the ban was lifted.

"You need me for anything else?" the man replied.

"Anyone look like they need a fix?"

"Yeah, the red head in bed five looked like she was jonesing."

"Alright, I'll check on her in a minute. You should head out; I'll call you when it's time to pick up Becky."

Javier watched the man leave and waited another five minutes before grabbing another black box from the safe. He checked the monitors, and sure enough, the red head in a bed off to the right was fidgeting and sweating.

He placed the box in his pocket and entered the room. Bed five sat fifteen feet away from Valentina. Javier knelt down on the bed and wiped the sweat from the woman's face.

"You doing okay?" he asked.

"I-I need a hit."

"But it's not time yet."

"Please, I need it."

"So, you want me to do you a favor?"

"Please, I'll do anything."

Javier unlatched the restraints and pulled the red head to her feet. He left the door open enough for the light to enter the room. "You need to prove how much you want it." He stroked his crotch with an evil grin on his face. He made it abundantly clear what he wanted, and the girl quickly complied.

She dropped to a knee, but he held her arm, preventing the red head from moving any further. He helped her to her feet and spun the woman around. He grabbed her waist and slammed his body into hers. There was enough light in the room to make them the focal point of every woman. Javier cast a glance over the red head's shoulder and saw Valentina was helplessly watching.

His hands traveled down the woman's arms before making their way to the bottom of her shirt. Slowly he peeled it off her body as he brought it over her head.

The woman stood in a pair of pink lace panties with her eyes closed. Her porcelain skin glistened with sweat as she remained the focal point of the room. Javier kissed her shoulders gently as his hands kneaded her exposed breasts. He moved slowly and sensually at first, but his thoughts turned towards Valentina as he caught her watching them.

He pinched the woman's budding nipples causing her to arch back and moan with delight.

"Tell me what you want from me," he whispered in her ear.

"I want you."

"What do you want?"

"I want your cock."

"Louder."

"I want your cock!"

"Good, now get on your knees and take it."

The red head complied. She dropped to her knees without hesitation and rubbed Javier's bulge. She pulled down his pants and stared at the large penis standing at attention. She licked her lips and kissed the tip.

Javier looked over at Valentina again as he grabbed a fistful of red hair, pulling the woman onto him. Her lips wrapped around his dick as he shoved it to the back of her mouth. He could feel her gag, but didn't care. He knew the red head gave the best blowjobs, but he was doing things his way; she was just there for the ride.

He pulled himself out just enough to feel her lips sucking the tip trying to hold him in. Javier smiled and thrusted himself deeper to the back of her throat. He did this repeatedly while keeping his eyes locked onto Valentina. He wanted her to watch. He wanted her to see what was in store for her.

The drugs he gave her already worked their way through her system. Javier knew she couldn't look away even if she wanted to. She was forced to watch as the red head sucked him off.

He began to imagine Valentina was the one on her knees in front of him. His desire to break her caused him to lose control. His grip loosened and the red head took over.

She alternated between jerking him off and licking his shaft slowly. She focused on the sensitive spot under the tip that caused Javier to shiver. He was nearly there before he realized the woman had taken control. He tightened his grip and shoved himself down her throat, thrusting harder and faster than before.

He locked eyes with Valentina one more time as he let out a guttural moan. He slammed his cock into the back of the woman's mouth again, but held her tightly as he filled her with his cum.

"Time for your reward," Javier whispered as he pulled the black box from his pocket. He administered the drug to the red head and ordered her back to bed. He was more than satisfied as he walked over to Valentina. "Hope you enjoyed the show." He scraped his finger along his shaft and wiped it along Valentina's lips. "Something for you to look forward to over the next few days."

There was no fight, no fire in her eyes. She was motionless as Javier did what he wanted to her, and there was nothing she could do to stop him.

Chapter 9-Ali

I spent the day watching every second of the airport footage from the time Valentina walked through the boarding gate to the time she was thrown into a white van. We watched it from every angle possible, and did so in silence. Lombardo jotted notes down every once in a while, but refused to speak unless he needed to have the video rewound, paused, or to resume play. Eventually, he was forced to discuss his cases a bit more in hopes they might help our investigation. Ricky seemed to believe the cases were connected, and that they tied to some human trafficking ring no one seemed to know about. I couldn't see how these were tied together other than all three were kidnapped, and all of them seemed to live in the Ulster County area.

By eight that night, I returned home. All I wanted was to see James, have a beer, and go to bed. I turned onto my block and saw a car parked in front of the house. I felt a smile spread across my face until I realized the vehicle didn't belong to James. I turned sharply into my driveway and jumped out of my car.

"Rodney, what the hell are you doing here?"

He exited the driver's seat and held up a six pack of beer. "Relax, I came bearing a gift."

I glared at him as I snatched one from his hand. "You mind telling me why you're at my house so late?"

The passenger side door opened, and out popped my five-foot-five lieutenant. "Ali, we need to talk."

I saw the pain and sadness in the lieutenant's eyes, and motioned for them to follow me inside the house. It was pitch black inside, which I've had a particular dislike for since Matthew's death. I rushed to turn on the nearest light, letting a soft orange glow cast over the living room.

"I'm guessing this is about your daughter," I said before the lieutenant could speak. "I haven't turned up much since yesterday. We know two men abducted her from the airport. Unfortunately, no matter what angle we viewed the video from; we never saw the men's faces. We learned she was thrown into the back of a white van, but there were no plates on it."

The lieutenant sank into the couch cushions downing a bottle. There was more I wanted to tell him, but I didn't know if he could handle hearing she may have been kidnapped as part of a human trafficking ring.

"So, who you working this case with?" Rodney asked.

"Lombardo," I replied with regret. I couldn't stand the man and everyone knew it. Just saying his name was like acid on my tongue.

Rodney chuckled while taking a swig from his bottle. "That should be fun," he said sarcastically. "I think you two will get along great."

"Fuck you, Rodney."

"Nah, you're not my type." He let out a loud laugh before chugging some more of his beer. "Hey, wasn't he working a missing persons' case?"

My eyes widened as I stared Rodney down. I tried to tell him to shut up telepathically, but that didn't seem to work. "Yeah, I guess so."

"Didn't he seem to think-"

"Rodney, you wanna help me in the kitchen for a minute?" I had to interrupt him. If he finished his thought, the lieutenant would know our working theory.

"What the hell you need me in the kitchen for?"

I walked over to him and slugged him in the gut. "Just do what I say."

"Okay," he gasped.

I practically had to drag Rodney out of the room. Once we were out of ear shot, I pulled him close and whispered, "Do not say a word. Lombardo's theory is the two missing girls were abducted into a human trafficking ring."

Rodney pulled back and took a deep breath. "Don't tell me you think the same men took Valentina?"

"That's what Ricky thinks."

"Who the hell is Ricky?"

"He's a friend who works for Port Authority. He helped get me on this case. Unfortunately, he assigned Lombardo as my partner."

"So he thinks she was abducted into this shit?"

"Yeah."

"And what do you think?"

"It's the only thing that makes sense at the moment. Tell me; has the lieutenant heard from the kidnappers?"

"No, nothing. That's why he's freaking out. He had me pick him up from his house and sat in the car with me for the last two hours waiting for you to get home."

"Rodney, you can't tell him anything I said to you."

"You think I wanna be the one to tell him this shit?"

"No, but you tend to have a big mouth."

"Screw you, Ali."

"What the hell are you two doing in there?" the lieutenant shouted.

"Trying to get Rodney to help me with dinner."

I could hear his beer bottle slam onto my coffee table. The lieutenant rounded the corner red faced and staring us down. "How can you think about food when my daughter is out there with god knows who?"

"Hey, a girl's gotta eat."

"You think this is funny?"

"No. I've been very serious about finding Valentina. But sitting around bitching and moaning about it isn't gonna help find her. You need to go home and let me do my job."

"Ali, there's no one else I would trust to find her."

"Then lay off and let me do what I need to do. I can't work her case twenty-four seven."

"I-I just don't what to do."

"You go home; be there for your wife, and console her while I track your daughter and her abductors down." I nodded to Rodney to signal him to take the lieutenant home. "If you don't mind, I need to grab some food and get some sleep so I can drive back to Queens tomorrow morning."

Rodney placed one of his massive hands on the lieutenant's shoulders and directed him towards the front door. "Goodnight, Ali," he said.

The lieutenant looked back. "Please find her," he pleaded.

"I will; I promise."

I sunk into a nearby chair the moment I heard the door close. I grabbed my beer and chugged the rest of it. It was nearly nine by the time Rodney and the lieutenant left. I had yet to eat and was already feeling my eyes getting heavy. I walked into the bedroom and kicked off my heels. There wasn't a sign of James or Amanda stopping home before I arrived. I just finished peeling my shirt and dress pants off when I heard the front door shut. My first thought was either James or Amanda came home, but the events of the previous year elevated my paranoia.

I grabbed my gun from the dresser and ran out of the bedroom, pointing it at the front door. I didn't find anyone standing there, but heard someone opening one of the bottles in the living room.

"Hello," I called out. I slowly crept around the corner and pointed my gun at the man sitting on my couch.

"Hello, gorgeous," James said while staring at me with lust in his eyes. "There's nothing hotter than seeing you in your bra and panties holding a gun. Oh wait; scratch that. Put on a sexy pair of heels with that outfit."

"You're such an ass," I replied while placing my gun on the mantle. I turned back towards the bedroom.

"Hey, where are you going?"

"To get changed."

"Why? You look great."

"I don't think I want to scar my sister if she decides to come home tonight and catches me walking around like this." I quickly pulled off the rest of my clothes and slipped into a pair of sweatpants and a t-shirt.

When I returned to the living room, James had already finished off one bottle. "How was your day?"

"It sucked. How about yours?"

"More or less the same. Did your lieutenant give you info on the case my captain mentioned?"

"Yeah," James said rather abruptly.

"Everything okay?"

He rolled his eyes as he reached for another beer. "I got a new partner, a bullshit case, and…" he trailed off as if he thought twice about finishing his sentence. "I really don't wanna talk about it."

"I understand." I sat down next to James on the couch and took one of the last two bottles.

"Did you find out anything on the lieutenant's daughter?"

"Not much." I told James what I uncovered and what Ricky told me earlier. James became rigid and concerned.

"Who are you working with on the case?"

"Ugh, Lombardo."

James shot up from the couch. "Are you fucking serious?"

"It's not a big deal."

"Not a big deal? That guy is a creep."

"Yeah, he is, but I can handle him."

"I don't trust him."

"You just don't like him because of the shit he said to me in the parking lot."

"No one talks to my girl like that. I should've knocked his ass out when I had the chance."

"Will you stop?"

"No, and if he crosses the line-"

"Then I will handle him. Trust me; I've been dealing with his shit for a while. If he crosses the line, I'll put him in his place. Now, you mind telling me what your case is about?"

The mere mention of his case caused James to become cold and distant. "It's a bullshit undercover case. The lieutenant wants me to go in as a potential client and infiltrate some company to expose some possible fraudulent activity."

"Undercover? This gonna be a daytime thing?"

"Days and nights. I don't really know when I'll be around until this case closes."

"I guess we'll just have to make the most of our time together."

"What did you have in mind?"

I straddled his lap and pulled his lips to mine. "I was thinking of something along those lines."

He grabbed my waist and hoisted me into his arms while my legs wrapped around his waist. "I like the way your mind works, Detective Ryan," James said with a smirk.

"Then you'll love what I have planned for you."

I tossed and turned all night thinking about Valentina. There was no telling where she was, who she was with, or what was happening to her, and that made me sick to my stomach.

I sat up for most of the night in the living room watching T.V. I must have passed out at some point, because the next thing I knew James was waking me up along with the orange glow of a sunrise.

"Hey, you been out here long?" he asked.

"Since one or two, I think. What time is it?"

It's six-thirty."

Well, so much for my morning run. I had just enough time to get ready and hit the road back to Queens. I propped myself back into a sitting position, leaving room for James to slip next to me. He pulled me closer.

"James, what are you doing?"

"We both have some time before work."

"Not that much time."

"Let me be the judge of that." He cupped my cheek with his hand and leaned in for a kiss. I felt the fire and electricity as his lips touched mine. The moment was short lived as the front door closed.

"Ew, you have a room; how about you use it?" Amanda said.

I pushed James back and jumped up from the couch. "So what; we're not allowed to kiss in our own house anymore?"

"You know what? It doesn't matter. I just came home to shower, change, and go to work."

"Yeah, where were you the last two nights?"

"Not like it's any of your business, but I was at my boyfriend's house." She stormed off down the hall and slammed her bedroom door.

"It is my business," I called through the door. "I'm your sister. And as long as you live in my house, I deserve to know if you're coming home or staying out all night."

Amanda opened the door and stared at me. "One, you're not my mother. I don't have to listen to you or let you know where I am every second of the day. Two, if I wanna spend the night with my boyfriend, I'm not calling you to ask your permission. And three, I won't be living under your roof for much longer." She pushed passed me and entered the bathroom.

"What do you mean?" I asked.

"Lucas asked me to move in with him last night."

"What did you tell him?"

"I told him I needed some time to think about it, but I'm strongly considering it."

"You're moving too fast. You've been dating him for what a month or two? You hardly know each other. I haven't even met him yet."

"You barely knew James before moving in with him."

"That was different. He was being a friend helping me through a dark time in my life."

"And he never thought about using it to fuck you?"

"Like I said; our situation was very different. "

"Yes, because Ali Ryan doesn't play by the same rules as everyone else. You think you're so special; why? Because you're the older sister or because you're the great Detective Ali Ryan?"

"I'm just trying to look out for you."

"No, you're trying to control my life." She swung open the bathroom door and stomped back to her room. She threw on her clothes quickly before scurrying towards the front of the house. "I'm done discussing this; I'm going to work."

I turned towards James who was making his morning coffee. "Can you believe her?"

He handed me a travel cup and kissed my cheek. "I'm sorry, but there's not much you can do about this."

"I'd just feel better if I met her boyfriend."

"So set up a double date with them and figure out if you like him."

"Brilliant. I knew there was a reason I loved you."

"Well, I would tell you to prove it, but you need to get on the road and I need to get ready for my case as well."

"Maybe if you're lucky I'll show you when we get home tonight."

He kissed my lips, his breath laced with the scent of coffee but in a way that reminded me how much I needed him. We desperately needed alone time, but with our case load, I didn't see that happening any time soon.

Chapter 10-HT

Javier sat in the chair with his eyes focused on the monitors. It was his job to watch over the girls, but he kept stealing glances at Valentina as she lay motionless on the bed. He wanted to go in there to check on her, but knew what it would look like if someone found him in the room with their newest acquisition. So, he remained the good employee and kept watch from a distance.

The door creaked open as the long haired Dimitri entered. "Shift change." Javier's head snapped towards him. "Yo, everything all right? You look out of it."

"Yeah, I'm fine."

"Man, you look like you're about to pass out. Go home and get some rest; I got this."

A part of Javier was grateful for the relief. He had been working for fifteen hours straight, but that didn't matter to him. He spent the majority of the day watching over Valentina, waiting for the boss to give him the green light. Seeing her every minute and not being able to touch her was self-inflicted torture.

"Alright, call me if you need anything," Javier said while expelling a deep breath. He exited the building and walked to the other side of the parking lot to a cluster of buildings. He unlocked the door and entered his apartment. It was a perk to have a rent-free home, but was also required of everyone working for his boss.

Javier understood the benefit. If anything should happen at the complex, they had enough men to take care of any situation. Being one of the top men, Javier had one of the nicest apartments.

He placed the keys on a small ash tray by the front door. He climbed a small set of stairs to his living room. His cat glanced up from the couch and let out a meow as she stretched out her black and white legs.

"Hey, furball, you miss me?"

The cat tilted her head to the side before rolling onto her back. Right on cue, Javier sat down next to the cat and began petting her chest. He picked up the remote and flipped through the channels, settling on an episode of Law and Order.

He felt himself relax for the first time in days. Loneliness was a feeling he embraced. The men he worked with were the closest people in his life, yet he never hung out with them or invited them over for a beer. Going out to stalk their targets were the only times he spent any time away from the complex. Their latest acquisition changed his world. He no longer wanted to hide in his apartment. He was drawn to Valentina, and wanted to make her his woman.

His thoughts became engulfed with the desire to feel her beneath him. He was too wrapped up in them, and missed a call from his boss. The ringing caught Javier's attention during the second attempt to reach him.

"Why didn't you pick up your phone?" the boss demanded.

"Sorry, sir. I was getting ready for bed and didn't hear it."

"You should know better than to step away from your phone. You never know when I need you."

"I'm assuming this is one of those times?"

"See, this is why you're one of my top men. Other than a missed call, you're always on top of your game. This is why I need you to run point tonight."

Javier closed his eyes and took a deep breath. "What's tonight?"

"Our shipping date has moved up. I need you to get the girls ready and escort them to the rendezvous."

"Which girls do you want me to bring?"

"I'll send the list to the office. You have two hours to get them ready and to arrive at the meet."

The line went dead. Javier was furious. He already worked fifteen hours and now had to escort a group of women to the shipment. He just prayed Valentina wasn't on the list. He doubted the boss had sold her off. She had only been in their custody for two days. It wasn't enough time to put her through the phases to break her, to make her obedient. But it would also be the smarter business move. The longer she stayed with them, the bigger the risk of the police tracking them down.

Javier rushed back to the office and found a list of five women the boss ordered him to bring to the meet. He had no idea how much they sold for, only they weren't Valentina.

"Dimitri," he called out when he entered the building. "I need your help to get the girls ready."

"You're sending them back out again?"

"No. The boss moved up the shipping date. We need to get them ready and out of here within the hour."

"You want me to go with you?"

"I need you to hold things down here. I'll take Theo with me."

Javier handed off the list to Dimitri and began waking the women. They were dragged from the dark dingy room and led to the showers. The men watched the ladies stand under the shower heads as water cascaded down their bodies. Dimitri stood off to the side stroking himself while he kept his eye on a skinny blond with a tight body. Javier barely acknowledged the women. Yes, they were beautiful, but they weren't what he wanted.

From the corner of his eye, Javier saw Dimitri take a step towards the shower. "Where are you going?"

Dimitri's eyebrow rose. "One last time couldn't hurt."

"Are you insane? The boss wants the girls ready and at the drop in an hour and a half. I don't think that includes fucking one of his girls."

"Hey, I won't see her again after tonight. I just wanna taste that pussy one more time. I want her to think of me when she's fucking some rich scumbag that thinks he owns her."

"You realize the boss will kill you if you touch her tonight?"

"It's not like I never fucked her before. Hell, he watched us a couple of times and filmed it."

"That was different. It was all about sex then; now it's business. You don't mess with his business no matter how bad you want a piece of that ass."

"Is that why you've been glued to the monitors the last couple days?"

"What are you talking about?"

"I see how you look at the new girl. You want her bad."

Javier slugged Dimitri in the arm. "It doesn't matter. She's off limits to everyone until the boss gives the all clear."

"So you do want her?"

"Just help me get the girls ready so I can get the fuck outta here. I'd like to get some sleep tonight."

The men turned off the water valve and ushered the women to another room, which few ever visited. Javier unlocked the door and brought the women inside. There were garment bags hung up with names written on tags, one for each girl. He unzipped the first and handed it to the blond Dimitri gawked at earlier.

"Make yourself useful and help her get dressed."

"Just give us five minutes alone."

"Give it a rest already. Her pussy isn't worth dying for."

Dimitri gritted his teeth, and grunted in anger. "Fine, I'll take her around the corner."

"Forget it; I got her. Go help the other girls get ready."

Javier grabbed the blond by the wrist and directed her to the back of the room. He handed her a bubble gum pink dress and sparkling silver sandals with a four inch heel. He took her back to the others and sat her in a chair.

Javier pressed a button to call their hair dresser. An old looking thirty-year-old entered into the room. The dark circles under her eyes and the aging lines on her showed the life she was forced to live. Javier remembered when she started working for them, although her employment was forced.

Rosie was taken from the mall five years earlier where she worked as a hairdresser and makeup artist. She caught the eye of their boss and decided he wanted her for himself. She was brought to the complex to be sold, but the boss decided her talents would've gone to waste. He made her a deal. She would be off limits to his men. In return, she would stay at the complex and work her magic on the other girls.

"Boss wants the girls looking their best," Javier said. "They need to be ready to be shipped out tonight."

Rosie looked at each girl and sighed, knowing the fate they would suffer once they left the complex. They all knew what was coming, but could do nothing to stop it.

It took the full hour to get all five girls ready. Javier led them to the white van where a beast of a man stood waiting. He towered over all with his thick six foot three frame. His long black hair fell to his shoulders making him look like a chocolate Adonis.

"Secure the women and let's go," Theo said.

Javier did as he was told and helped each woman into the back of the van. He didn't need to worry about them trying to escape. Each were given a small injection, just enough to give them a high, but not enough to make them too drugged to function.

They drove to a warehouse and unloaded the women. They waited in silence for another twenty minutes before the first of the buyers appeared. He looked to be in his fifties, dressed in an Armani suit. His smiled turned Javier's stomach as he approached. This wasn't his first encounter with the man.

He was known only as Mr. M. and had been a frequent buyer, four women to be exact. Once the girls left, they were never heard from again. Javier was sure he used them until he no longer wanted them. What he did after was unknown.

He approached the brunette in a red dress. He grabbed her hand and kissed the back of it. "You are such a beauty. I will spend every day cherishing you."

Theo took a step forward and handed Mr. M. a thin black bag containing a new ID and passport. It was the essentials the buyers needed to help the women start a new life.

Mr. M. placed a hand on the small of the woman's back and led her from the building. They didn't have to worry about the buyers turning on them. The money was wirelessly transferred prior to the meet. The girl wouldn't have been marked on the list unless the boss received payment in advance.

One-by-one the buyers showed up to the warehouse to pick up their package until Javier was left with the blond Dimitri was obsessed with. He thought about his partner's infatuation with the woman, and considered the possibility Dimitri was in love with her. He was desperate to be with her one last time. It made Javier wonder what would've happened if he let them go off on their own. Would it have just been sex, or would he convince her to run away with him?

Those were dangerous thoughts to have considering how much he wanted Valentina. Being forced to keep himself at bay only made him want her more.

He watched the final buyer arrive and take the blond away. He pictured what it would be like to see Valentina walk off with another man. There was an ache in his chest he had never felt before.

"Can we get the fuck outta here? I need to get some sleep," Javier said. But he knew it would be impossible to sleep with his thoughts seeking a future he could never have with a forbidden woman.

Chapter 11-Ali

I showed up at the Port Authority office early to get a jump start on Valentina's case. Imagine my surprise when I found Lombardo sitting in the room buried deep in case files.

"What the hell are you doing here so early?" I asked.

"I could ask you the same question."

"Well, I asked you first."

He shook his head and rolled his eyes at me. Yeah, I know; we were acting like school kids. All we needed was for one of us to call the other a name and respond with I know what you are but what am I.

"I'm not here for you to bust my balls. I'm here to solve these cases and hopefully find these missing girls."

"And you don't think I am?"

"No. You wanna sit here and be a bitch instead of finding a way to work together. The lieutenant's daughter is your top priority and you hope to find the other girls along the way."

"You're damn right Valentina is my priority. You know as well as I do the first forty-eight hours are the most crucial in a missing person's case. We're about to hit that mark today."

"So you think she's more important than finding these girls that have been missing for weeks?"

"No, but I think if you guys are right, and she was abducted by these human trafficking assholes, locating Valentina is our best shot at finding the rest of the missing girls."

"You're both right," Ricky said as he entered the room. "Valentina is our best chance at finding the missing girls. But the other cases are equally as important. We need to examine all three women; what they did in their spare time; where they went; who they dated; who they hung out with. We need something that can link them together to see what made our suspect choose them."

"You mean like criminal profiling?" I asked.

"Yes, exactly," Ricky replied.

"Sounds like somebody has been watching too many cop shows on T.V." Lombardo folded his arms across his chest and met my eyes with a smirk.

"What if I do?" I snapped.

Lombardo shrugged his shoulders. "Nothing wrong with it; I'm just saying you sounds like you watch a lot of them."

His words hid the comments he wanted to make, but was too much of a coward to say them to my face. Me on the other hand, I was brutally honest whether you were my friend or enemy.

"Maybe you should watch some; you might learn something."

"Enough," Ricky shouted. "We're not going to get anywhere with you two bickering at each other all day. Now, you both need to put whatever issues you have aside and focus on the case. I think we need to focus on the two cases Detective Lombardo was working on to see if anything sticks out."

I hated to be overruled, but the choice wasn't mine to make. Ricky was put in charge of Valentina's case. If we weren't careful, there was a chance all three of us would be removed from it.

"Fine," I said through gritted teeth. "Lombardo, what else can you tell us about the missing girls?"

"The first missing girl was nineteen from Queens. She went to school in New Paltz. According to her friends, she was studying to become a teacher with an emphasis in English. She was also a runner on the track team."

"If she was a runner, I doubt the suspects took her like they did Valentina. She would've been able to outrun them."

"Unless she knew them," Ricky interrupted. "They may have known each other from campus or met on the bus and became friendly enough where she let her guard down."

"Both are very possible scenarios, but that still wouldn't make sense for her not to run the moment she sensed danger."

"Maybe they didn't raise any red flags for her until it was too late." Ricky glanced back at Lombardo. "Tell us more about victim number two."

"Tina was a straight A student who just graduated high school. She lived in Highland but was planning on going away to college in Pennsylvania. She was set to leave the week after she was reported missing."

I held up a hand to stop Lombardo from speaking. "You said yesterday she was last seen at a party, right?"

"Yeah, on Grove Street."

"So both of your victims were last seen in New Paltz?"

"We don't know for sure Ms. Gutierrez made it to New Paltz before she was taken, but that is the working theory."

"Ali, what's going on? What's that brain of yours working on?"

"Valentina lived in the Ulster County Area. That would indicate all three girls lived in same county. That means our suspects must be living in the area as well."

"We can work with that assumption," Ricky said. "But we still need to consider they may only be targeting women in New Paltz due to it being a college town. They could be hiding out and holding the women anywhere."

Lombardo massaged the temples on his head. "I hate to admit this, but I think she's on to something." My jaw nearly dropped after hearing his words. "I think we all can agree the two missing girls were abducted from New Paltz." We all nodded in agreement. "I pressed hard with my investigation. Shortly after, the lieutenant's daughter was taken from the airport and they called him personally to threaten him. Why?"

"Because your investigation stirred up a hornet's nest, which provoked them to do something drastic to back him off." For once, Lombardo and I agreed on something.

"So you're both thinking they did this to scare off your lieutenant?"

"No," I replied. "They did this to piss him off enough to make him desperate enough to make a mistake, one that would force the whole station to stay away from the case."

"But how would that stop me from investigating these two cases?" Lombardo held up two folders and slapped them back down on the table.

"I don't think that was their plan. If they are selling the girls, they may try to move them soon making it nearly impossible to find them."

Ricky kept his back towards us. His anger radiated throughout the room. He knew I was right, which meant we were running out of time.

"You two need to focus all your attention on these missing girls." He moved towards the exit and flung open the door.

"Where are you going?" I asked.

"I'm calling in a favor of my own."

Chapter 12- Ali

I returned home around nine that night. Truthfully, I would've stayed there all night if I thought it would help us get further in our investigation. I spent ten hours pouring over every bit of information we had on the three missing girls, and didn't seem to be any closer to finding them than I was when I first arrived that morning. I was happy to be rounding the corner of my block. I wanted nothing more than to slip out of my clothes and into James' arms.

As I crept closer to my house, I saw more cars than usual lined up along the street, four of them to be exact. I pulled into my driveway and glanced back to see if anyone was still in their vehicle. Once I saw no one there, I marched up to the front door. My immediate thought was to kill my sister for having people over without telling me. That all changed when I entered the house.

There were three men, a black and red haired woman, and my boyfriend sitting around the living room, talking loudly and animatedly until I entered the room.

"Ali," James said in a tone of surprise. "You're home."

Two of the men jumped to their feet to greet me. I recognized them from when they helped James move into the house. There was a tall black male with glasses, named Josh. He was a techie type of guy from what James told me, and could put most hackers to shame. The other was a well built, stocky man named Brad. He did most of the lifting during moving day. He didn't look it, but the man was strong as an ox.

"Hi Ali," Josh said with a big smile on his face as he leaned in for a hug. I forgot how much Josh towered over me. He needed to bend down several inches for his eyes to meet mine.

"Hi Josh…Brad…What are you guys doing here?"

"Your boy needed some help and called us for our expertise," Brad replied as he leaned in to embrace me.

"So he begged you guys and called in a favor?"

"More like he added to the laundry list of favors he owes us."

"Anything I can help with?"

James got up from the couch and stood next to me. "Sorry, Ali. They're helping me with the case I was assigned."

"So you can call in four civilians, but not your girlfriend who's a detective?" I shot him a sideways glance.

"Not quite. Josh and Brad are helping with some surveillance work."

"And what about the other two?"

"The bald headed son of a bitch sitting down is my new partner. Detective Ali Ryan, meet Officer Marconi."

"That's Detective Marconi, asshole." The stocky, bald-headed man stood up to shake my hand. He locked eyes with James and stared him down. I could feel the tension between them. It didn't seem like either was happy to be working with each other. Knowing James, he probably worked with the man before and pissed him off being his typical arrogant self. "Please tell me you put this jackass in his place."

"Oh I do. I may have to do so again once everyone leaves."

"You got popcorn? I'd love to watch that show."

"I'll record it and let you play it at the station. I mean why should you get all the fun of watching me put his balls in my purse?"

Marconi laughed and walked back to his chair. "I like this one. Please tell me you're gonna marry this one."

"Shut the fuck up, Marconi," James growled.

"Hey, be nice to your partner. He's a guest in our house."

"Yeah, be nice to me."

James didn't seem to be thrilled with his new partner and being friendly with me set him on edge even more. But I couldn't help notice the woman sitting on the couch. Her eyes were staring daggers at me from the moment I entered the living room, and barely turned away from me. James didn't attempt to introduce us. Maybe it was for the best. But then again, when did I ever do what was best for me?

I approached the woman and stuck out my hand. "Hi, I'm Ali...James' girlfriend." Yeah, I felt the need to stake my claim in front of this woman. She looked hot, seemed like she had a pretty fit body, and had been sitting a little too close to James on the couch. Add the fact she'd been giving me the stink eye, and my claws were ready to come out.

"The name's Joselyn."

I froze in my tracks at the sound of her name. My head snapped back to look at James. He averted his eyes, confirming this was the same Joselyn he used to date. I didn't know why she was sitting in my house or why she was anywhere near James. I just knew I wanted to knock the smirk off her face.

"Nice to meet you. James told me virtually nothing about you."

"Funny, he didn't mention anything about a girlfriend either."

"I think we're done for the night," James quickly said, trying his best to separate the two of us before someone pushed the other too far. "We can meet back at the station tomorrow."

Brad and Josh must have understood what James was attempting and quickly said their goodbyes. Marconi sat back in his chair smiling, almost egging us to carry on.

"Go before I throw your ass out," James snapped.

"But this is just getting good."

James ripped Marconi out of the chair and shoved him towards the door. He glanced back at Joselyn and nodded for her to follow. She jumped up and sauntered up to James. She slowly leaned in and brushed her lips against his cheek while whispering something in his ear. She looked back at me one more time before raising an eyebrow and walking out the front door.

I waited until we were alone before grilling James. "You mind telling me what that was all about?"

"It's not what you think."

"You don't know what I'm thinking."

"I know you're thinking Joselyn is trying to make a play for me."

"No, not really. It was more like if she's stupid enough to try something, I'll break her pretty little face."

"Ali, there's nothing going on between us. Joselyn's only here because of the investigation."

"How is she part of it exactly? I mean, she's not a cop and she doesn't really seem like she has a set of skills that would help solve a case."

"Joselyn uncovered some evidence that linked the company she works for with ponzi scheme. She brought it to my lieutenant's attention and he ordered me to work the case."

"You mean she asked for you to be part of the investigation?"

"According to my lieutenant, Joselyn came to him and presented him the info asking not to include me."

"And why would she add that request?"

"Because the last time she was part of my investigation, the woman I loved was murdered."

"Wait…what?"

"It's a long story, one that still haunts me."

"You wanna talk about it?"

James shook his head while moving towards the couch. "No, not yet."

I inched closer to console him. James never really told me about the cases he worked before he met me. Having lost someone he loved, explained why he changed the subject any time I brought it up.

As I extended my hand towards his shoulder, the front door opened. Amanda entered, apparently trying to slip by unnoticed.

"Where have you been?" I asked.

"I was out."

"With who?"

"A friend."

"Which friend?"

"Not like it's any of your business, but I was with my boyfriend."

"You should've invited him inside to meet us."

"Why; so you could ask him fifty million questions like you're doing to me right now?" Amanda stormed off towards her room.

"Sorry if I want to know who my little sister is dating."

"No, you're being nosey. You want to interrogate my boyfriend to see if he measures up to your standards."

"With everything that's happened, I'd like to know you're with someone that'll treat you right and not some psycho."

"Yeah, well…I already have a mother. I don't need another one." I watched Amanda disappear into her room and slammed the door shut.

James met me in the hall, wrapping one of his arms around my waist. He pulled me close and kissed my cheek. "She doesn't need a protector. I think Amanda needs to live her life away from our chaotic lives."

"You think this is my fault?"

"No, but Amanda isn't meant for the cop life. And lately, we brought a whole lot of crazy home. I think it might've been too much for her and she needs to find a more normal life."

"So you want her to move out?"

"I think she needs to do what's best for her and so do we."

"What's that supposed to mean?"

"I think we need to keep our minds on solving these cases so we can finally focus on us." He turned to enter our bedroom.

I understood what he meant. In the short time we were together, most of it was spent looking over our shoulders while hunting a psychopath who was hell-bent on destroying my life. We were in desperate need to have some alone time and it didn't seem like we would get it any time soon.

James pulled me to the bedroom, but heard my cell ringing before the door closed. I quickly grabbed the phone and answered. "This is Ryan."

"Ali, it's Ricky. Can you talk?"

I glanced at James and mouthed the words *I'm sorry*. I exited the bedroom and walked back to the kitchen. "What's up?"

"I might have a lead on the missing girls' case."

"Really? How? What did you find?"

"I called in some favors this afternoon. One of them does some security work for different warehouses, office buildings and occasionally does some work as a bouncer. He lives up in your neck of the woods and so I mentioned the case to him."

"What did he say?"

"He hasn't noticed anything unusual at the bars in Poughkeepsie, but he has noticed a car driving around one of the warehouses he watches over."

"You think our guys are using this warehouse for their operation?"

"I don't know, but it's worth investigating. I can text you his info if you wanna talk to him."

"Absolutely. Can I meet him tonight?"

"I figured you'd request to speak to him immediately. He told me where he's patrolling tonight. Take Lombardo with you for protection."

"I don't need a babysitter or protection. I can take care of myself."

"I know you can, but I'd feel better knowing you had someone there watching your back."

"I promise; my partner will be there tonight." I hung up with Ricky and scrolled through my contacts list. "Hey, partner, I need you to get your ass over to my house and pick me up."

"Ali, do you know what time it is?" Rodney asked.

"It's about the lieutenant's daughter. I might have a lead."

"Alright, I'll be right there."

It didn't take Rodney long to arrive at my house. I slipped out before James realized I left. "Drive," I demanded the instant I jumped into the passenger seat.

"You mind telling me where we're going?"

"Ricky called one of his contacts that happens to work as a security guard. He thinks he might be able to help with the investigation."

"You tell this to Lombardo?"

My cheeks turned a light shade of red as I refused to answer. Instead, I gave him directions to the warehouse and sat in silence while waiting for the next turn.

After ten minutes, Rodney decided to approach the subject. "You know he's gonna be pissed at you for leaving him out."

"Ricky gave me the lead and I needed to move on it fast. Besides, this is my investigation, not his."

"I thought the captain assigned you both to it."

"Hey, if I wanted to argue all night, I would've brought Lombardo. Right now, I need someone to watch my back."

"Damn, girl; I'm just looking out for ya."

"I know, but that's not what I need."

He remained quiet for the duration of the drive until we pulled into a parking lot. Only one car sat in the lot facing the road. In the distance was a small warehouse, which seemed small, compared to others I've seen in the area. We pulled up alongside the car and rolled down the window.

"Excuse me; are you Victor Sims?" I asked.

"Detective Ryan?"

I showed him my badge. "Ricky told me you had some information that could help us with our investigation."

"I don't know much, but I've noticed the same car pull into this lot every night. They drive around the building and then stop at the front door. The moment I started my engine, they took off."

"You think someone's casing the joint?" Rodney asked.

"Maybe, but last night I saw several cars parked in the back of the warehouse. I called it in to my supervisor."

"You didn't call the police?" I asked.

"I started to, but everyone left before I could reach an operator."

I was getting a bad feeling the deal happened and we were too late. Our only hope was that Victor saw something that could identify any of the men.

"Did you happen to see anyone?"

"No. Like I said, I patrolled the area and found the cars. I called it in and then they were gone."

"Were you able to get any info on the vehicles they were driving; license plate numbers, color, or the make and model?"

"I think one was a town car, one was a limo, there was a white van, and a couple others I've never seen before."

My eyes darted to Rodney at the mention of the white van. He nodded and must have had the same thought I did; *we were too late.*

Chapter 13-HT

Javier spent most of the day recuperating after the long night. He was restless. He was used to supervising the women being transferred, but it was different when he saw the woman Dimitri cared about be sold to the highest bidder. He barely acknowledged anyone when he returned to the complex. Instead, he called the boss to let him know everything went off without a hitch and returned to his apartment.

His thoughts lingered on the moment the blond walked off. Javier imagined it was Valentina. He knew it was only a matter of time before she was listed on a shipment and sold to be a sex slave for some rich asshole who would destroy her mentally and emotionally while using her body for their own pleasure. He couldn't imagine watching her get dragged away into that life.

He was woken by the sound of his phone ringing. He picked it up before missing the second call. "Hello," he mumbled.

"Wake up, sleepy head. You've got work to do."

Hearing the voice of his boss caused him to jump from the bed. He rushed to grab clothes from the closet. "What do you need?"

"You can start by meeting me at the office."

"Yes, sir. I'll be there in a twenty minutes." He showered and dressed himself quickly before walking across the parking lot to the office. The building was secured by a keycard access locks. Only a few trusted men were provided that privilege.

Javier entered the office, finding Dimitri standing in front of the desk. Neither man would lock eyes with the other as they stood before the boss.

"You called for me, sir?"

"We need more recruits for our next shipment. We have three including that cop's daughter. We need more."

"With all due respect," Javier said. "As long as we have her, all of this is in jeopardy. Her father and those cops won't stop until they hunt us down and get her back."

"I admire your concern, but we did this knowing it would piss them off. They'll make a mistake and be forced to back off. By the time someone else steps up to take their place, we will have sold every woman and have made enough money to disappear."

"You really think moving forward is a good idea?"

Dimitri's head turned towards Javier with a look of hatred and amusement.

"Don't tell me you're going soft on us," the boss said.

"No, sir. I was just being cautious."

"I believe that's part of my job. You two just focus on getting another couple of girls for the next shipment. I suggest you get started tonight. Will that be a problem?"

"No, sir," Javier replied.

The boss glanced back at Dimitri. "What about you?"

"I'm all set. Can we take any of them for a test drive?"

"Be my guest." Dimitri had a smile on his face, but Javier tried to mask his look of disgust. "Now, I expect you guys have a long night ahead of you, and I have a few last minute meetings to attend to."

The boss exited the office leaving his two men behind. "You look like shit," Dimitri said.

"Oh like you look any better?"

"It wasn't a good night."

Javier assumed Dimitri didn't get much sleep after losing his blond fuck toy. But he could see through the charade. Javier knew the woman meant more to Dimitri than he let on.

"You okay?" he finally asked.

"Yeah, I'll be fine." Dimitri shrugged his shoulders and walked towards the door. "It's nothing that a blowjob from a dumb drunk bitch at the bar won't cure."

Javier believed it was a front. He doubted Dimitri would go through with a bar hook up the night after losing the woman he cared about. It didn't matter, none of it did. They had their orders. They were to find some new girls for their boss, and they needed to be worth enough to satisfy their clients.

They drove out to New Paltz and parked a block off from Main Street. They knew the boss wanted someone young, and targeting a college town was perfect for fulfilling the request. Lucky for them, it was Thursday…bar night. Most of the students walked from campus looking for a party. It gave Javier and Dimitri plenty of bars and women to choose.

They targeted a bar the students called Cabs. It was one where students under the age of twenty-one were able to get in for college night. It was the perfect place to begin their night. It was the easiest way to find a couple of young girls that would be more than happy to let two guys buy them drinks. They were the easy marks. They were the girls that would think two random guys giving them free drinks when they were underage was a great idea.

They walked down the alley to the bar and showed their IDs. It was dark inside but the men were quickly engulfed in multi-colored spotlights that bounced off the walls. There were more students packed in the building than the men realized, and could barely move.

"Let's get out of here," Javier suggested.

"Why? We just got here."

"You really think we're gonna find a pair of girls in here?"

"I can get a chick anywhere. I picked up that one girl at the Stop N Shop last month. I worked my magic, helped her bring her groceries home, and fucked her for hours. I probably could've gone a second round if it wasn't for the boss calling me."

"Prove it."

The men scoured the bar looking for their conquests, but found it more difficult than they originally thought. Most of the girls they liked were surrounded by a group of friends with several men sniffing around looking to make their moves.

Javier really didn't care. He was forced to be there and had no interest in picking up some random bar chick. He was hoping Dimitri would do the dirty work for him and would call it a night. He stood at the edge of the dance floor glancing around the room. When he turned towards Dimitri, he realized his cohort was missing.

He decided staying where he was would be the best option, thinking Dimitri left to grab a drink. After ten minutes, he became worried and started searching for him, wondering if Dimitri was off doing something stupid.

He walked all around the bar, but only found a pair of girls that were annoyed at how long it took to get a drink. He listened to them talk about going to another bar and their options. They walked back to the entrance with Javier trailing far behind. He bumped into a guy leaving the bathroom.

"Fuck, dude; where the hell were you," Javier asked.

"I was out proving you wrong."

"What?"

"Just got a blowjob in the bathroom by some chick I met. I guess that just proves I can get laid anywhere I want."

"That's great; can we re-focus on why we're here tonight?"

Dimitri shrugged his shoulders and looked around. "You see anyone you like? The one I had was alright, but not the quality the boss requested."

"I saw two girls a few minutes ago talking about leaving here and going over to Cuddy's."

"You wanna head over there?"

"Faster we pick them up, the quicker we can be done with tonight."

"Why; so you can go back to staring at some stupid girl through the monitor? At least tonight you can shove your dick in some bitch and get off for a change."

Javier knew Dimitri made sense on some level. He never needed convincing to enjoy bar night. It wasn't until he met Valentina that he second-guessed himself. But what else could he do? She was still off limits to him and all the rest of the guys at the complex.

"Shut the fuck up and let's go find those chicks."

They left Cabs and headed back towards Main Street. They followed the road until they reached Cuddy's. There weren't many people inside, which made it more difficult to put their plan in motion. There was no way they could get the girls out of there without someone noticing two sober guys carrying two drunk girls out of a bar.

They entered and took a spot to the right of the girls. They ordered a couple of beers and moved to the pool table. The men kept their eyes on the girls as they took turns shooting around. They weren't serious about the game, but used it as a way to keep watch and to count how many drinks the girls had.

After the second round, Dimitri made his way back to the bar and started to talk to the young red head. He nodded back towards Javier while ordering another round. The girls conversed for a moment before joining Javier and Dimitri at the table.

"Ladies, this is my friend Javier. He's a bit shy, but I'm sure he'll warm up to you in a bit." He gestured to the brunette while continuing the introductions. "Javi, this is Brenda and Sandy."

"Nice to meet you." Javier saluted them with his nearly empty bottle before taking the last gulp and slamming the drink on the table. "You play?"

"Not really," Sandy replied. "But I'm sure I'll be a pro if someone shows me how to work the stick." She cocked her head to the side and stared at Dimitri.

Javier knew Sandy belonged to Dimitri that night, which meant he was on Brenda watch. "What about you?"

"I've played a bunch of times. My brother used to play on a team and showed me everything he knew."

That was going to be a problem if the guys planned on using the game to get the girls more drunk, but Dimitri must not have heard her comment. "I say we make this interesting. How about a shot per ball sunk?"

Brenda smiled and agreed. They let me break, sinking the three ball in the right corner pocket. That caused Brenda to take a shot. She raised her eyebrows before placing the glass to her lips. The amber liquid was gone in a second. Javier smiled, taking his eyes off the ball and missed his next shot.

"My turn," Brenda said as she took her spot at the other end of the table. She surveyed her options and methodically cleared half the striped balls. "I told you my brother taught me everything he knew."

Javier walked back to the table to retrieve the four shots. "You're an asshole," he said as the red head nipped at Dmitri's ear.

"Relax; you'll thank me later."

Javier downed the drinks just as Brenda finished her run on the table. She grabbed her beer and took a swig. "You're up."

Dimitri slipped out from under Sandy and demolished most of the solids. He smirked at the red head with the fuck me eyes, and scratched with one ball left.

"You're turn, gorgeous."

Sandy took her spot and barely connected the cue ball with one of the stripes. By the time she returned to the table, Dimitri had pushed two shots to the edge.

Javier had an easy time knocking the last solid into the side pocket before giving him the perfect shot on the eight ball to end the game. The girls took the two shots Dimitri kept in front of him and downed every bit of its contents.

They spent another twenty minutes playing around the pool table, finishing the remaining shots and another round of beers. The girls were becoming more flirtatious, including Brenda who was more reserved than Sandy.

"I think it's time we head out, maybe take this party somewhere more private," Dimitri suggested.

The girls barely acknowledged what was said and were already leaning on the guys for support. Javier looked down at Brenda and back at Dimitri. He had a glassy look to his eyes, the same glassy look the girls had.

"What the fuck, man?"

"I told you; you'll thank me later. Now, let's get the girls out of here and have some real fun."

Dimitri led the group down the road to the van. He helped Javier and the girls into the back while he drove down Route 299 to the nearest motel. He left the trio in the van to go check-in. He returned shortly after and brought them to the room. He took Sandy to the closest bed, while Javier stumbled to the other bed with Brenda at his side.

They fell to the bed as the drugs took its full effect on Javier. There was nothing he could do, the drug and alcohol had mixed together and was coursing throughout his body. He could barely move, but felt Brenda playing with him. The room quickly became a blur as his eyelids became heavy. The last thing he heard was the sounds of both women moaning as the room faded from sight.

Chapter 14-Ali

I slept on the couch still seething from the night before. I was pissed about the case. The first solid lead and we were a day late. I didn't know if Valentina had been sold to some slime-ball or if they still had her in their custody. It didn't matter; I needed to keep pursuing the investigation. I planned on finding the kidnappers and making them pay for what they did to Valentina.

I rolled onto the floor and scrambled to my feet. I had to shower and get ready for work, but didn't want to wake James. I crept into the bedroom and found the bed empty. *Did he already leave?*

I listened for any sound, but the house was too quiet for my liking. I had become too used to people being around watching T.V., playing music, or talking. I was usually lost in thought about a case, but my mind was stuck on the empty house and what happened the night before. Seeing his ex sitting smugly on my couch sparked a hateful rage I didn't know existed. I wanted nothing more than to knock that smirk off her face. I held back because of James, but that would've been different had he not been there.

He never leaves without saying goodbye. I wondered if it was retaliation for sneaking out without telling him where I was going. I had no choice. If he knew where I was going, he would have invited himself, or worse, followed us to the warehouse. Truthfully, Rodney shouldn't have been there either. He was ordered to stay away from the case by the captain, but Ricky wanted someone to go with me and I didn't trust Lombardo.

I took a quick shower and entered the kitchen to make a cup of coffee. The pot was cold and no coffee had been made. Damn, how mad must James have been to leave without having his morning brew?

I thought about calling him to make sure he was okay, but I didn't want to be a pain in the ass. He already thought I was overprotective of my sister. Maybe I was, but I deserved to meet the man she was dating. After everything we were put through over the last year and a half, I found it difficult to trust anyone.

I knocked on Amanda's door to ask if she wanted any coffee. There was no response. I tried again, but was met with silence. "Hey, I just wanted to apologize for last night. I'm sorry if I've been overreacting. I'm just a bit paranoid after the last few cases." She still didn't respond. Usually, she would jump at the opportunity to revel in my apologies, but she wasn't at that moment. I knocked one last time. "Amanda, are you up?" I opened the door to find an empty bed.

It was only six-thirty and I was at home alone. The rate I was going, sitting in an empty house seemed like my future. That thought sent me into a panic, causing me to reach for my phone. I needed to talk to them…James or Amanda. The moment I touched my cell, it began ringing.

"This is Ryan."

"Hey." It was a familiar low grumbling male voice.

"Lombardo, is that you?"

"No, it's the friggin pizza man."

"What the fuck do you want? How'd you get my number?"

"Got it from the lieutenant. I talked it over with Ricky last night, and we agreed to talk to the friends and roommates of the two missing girls. I figured you might wanna talk to them yourself." I hated to admit it, but Lombardo had a good idea.

"Was that all you two discussed?"

"Yeah, why?"

"No reason. Give me a half hour and I'll meet you in New Paltz."

I drove around campus for a half hour looking for Lombardo. The son of a bitch told me to meet him at the dorms on campus, but never told me which one. I pulled into the commuter lot in the back by the dorm Amanda used to live in, and found the giant ass leaning against his Jeep.

"Where the hell have you been?" he asked with a smug look on his face. He knew damn well why it took me so long to find him.

"Next time you wanna meet somewhere, you might wanna be a little more specific about the place."

"Hey, I told you to meet me at the dorms on campus."

"Do you realize how many dorms there are here?

"How the hell would I know?"

"Because you conducted an investigation on two missing girls. One of them lived on campus."

"The only people I talked to lived in that dorm over there, the one across from it, and a house a few blocks away."

"And you couldn't remember the names of the dorms?"

Lombardo shrugged his shoulders. "It's in the case report. I was in a hurry and decided this morning it would be better to have you here helping me."

I wanted to go off on him for considering me an afterthought, but at least he asked me to help him talk to those closest to the missing girls. I could easily stay and argue, but we were already working against the clock.

"Do you at least remember the room numbers of the students you spoke to?" He handed me a slip of paper with a name, hall name and room number. "You realize the name of the dorm was written on here?"

"Oh, it was?" His smirk clearly indicated he omitted the information on purpose. It was his way of doing the right thing by including me in his investigation while still finding a way to be a jackass.

"Fuck you. Let's find the girls and see if they remembered anything since the last time you talked to them."

We split up. Lombardo took the closer of the two dorms, leaving me with Estrada Hall. I knocked on the door and waited for someone to come close enough for me to show them my badge. I entered and was met with the familiar sight of maroon plush chairs. I remembered staring at them the day I heard of Rachel Walker's death. At the time, I only knew it as an accidental overdose at the dorm. I panicked and thought it was Amanda. I had freaked out and waited nervously in front of the elevator, only to see my sister emerging from the heavy metal doors.

This time, I wasn't nervous. I was there with a purpose. I stood waiting for the same elevator to take me to Katrina Gutierez's room, hoping her roommate would remember something that could help us.

I followed the hall on the second floor to room 208. The girl obviously didn't know she was being visited by the police. She stood in a pink Hello Kitty shirt and beige shorts. Her hair was disheveled and her eyes were half closed.

"Ms. Clarke?" I asked.

"Yeah," the girl mumbled.

"I'm Detective Ryan with the Ulster County Police Department. I'd like to speak with you about your roommate, Katrina Gutieriez."

Her eyes opened wide as she stared at me. "I-I spoke to another officer about her. I told him everything I could remember about that night."

"This is just a follow up. We're inclined to believe this wasn't just a random disappearance or kidnapping."

"What are you saying?"

I glanced over her shoulder at the large lump in her bed. "I think it's better if you ask your guest to leave before we continue this conversation."

She blushed and walked back into the room, letting the door close behind her. A few minutes later, the man from her bed exited and held the door for me to enter. The roommate had pulled her hair back into a ponytail and turned on the lights in the room.

"Sorry about that, detective."

"It's alright. I remember what college life is like."

The glare in her eyes seemed like she questioned how long ago that was. "Like I said before, I told that other detective everything I knew."

"I'm sure, but please indulge me. You never know what little tidbit of information you may have overlooked in the past."

She shrugged her shoulders and sat down on her bed. "Be my guest."

"When was the last time you saw Katrina?"

"I drove her to the bus station on Main Street so she could go home for the weekend."

"And did you hear from her after that?"

"She called me that Sunday to let me know when she was supposed to be back. We arranged for me to pick her up that night."

"Did she call or text you during the ride back?"

"Nope. Her bus was due to arrive around seven. I waited until eight before I got worried and started calling and texting her. By nine I went down to the station and started asking if there was a delay."

"And what did they say?"

"The bus showed up on time. I tried calling her again after that, but it went straight to voicemail. I figured she might've met someone and didn't want to be bothered. So I went back to the dorm and turned in for the night. I called her after my first class but got her voicemail again."

"Did she ever text you to let you know she was on the bus?"

"Um yeah, I think so."

"Can you pull up your last texts from her?"

She reached onto the nightstand and grabbed her phone. After a minute of scrolling, she handed me her cell. "Yeah she sent me this before she left."

Getting on the bus. Should be home around seven.

That ruled out the possibility of Katrina being taken before stepping foot on the bus. It left me with two scenarios; either her kidnapper was on the bus or the kidnapper was waiting at the bus station for her. There was one thing I needed to know; did Katrina know her abductor?

"Was Katrina very friendly and outgoing?"

"Yeah, absolutely."

"Was she the kind of girl that made friends fast?"

"Yeah, you could say that I guess."

"Was she the type of person that would talk to random strangers?"

"It depends on the situation. If she met them in class, on campus or at a party, then yes. But she wouldn't strike up a conversation with some random person on the street."

"What about on a bus?"

"No, she usually listened to music and slept during her trips."

"What about at a party?"

"If a guy was hot enough, she'd talk to them, but never went home with a guy if that's what you're implying."

"I'm not implying anything, Ms. Clarke. I'm merely trying to understand Katrina a little better." I jotted a note on a piece of paper and looked back up at the roommate. "When was the last time she met someone at a bar or party?"

"I think she mentioned some guy the week before she went home."

I perked up after hearing that. "Do you remember anything about this guy; what he looked like; where they met?"

"I never saw the guy. Katrina told me they met at Oasis, I think."

"Was this mentioned to the other officer?"

"No, he never asked and I didn't think of it until now."

I gave her a knowing look that said I was right. "Did Katrina talk to this guy after that night?"

"I don't think so. I never asked to be honest."

"Do you remember seeing anyone hanging around that was a bit out of place or seemed to be watching Katrina?"

"No, she usually hung out with the same people all the time."

It wasn't much to go on, but it was enough to give me a slight lead in the case. "Thank you, Ms. Clarke. Here's my card if you can think of anything else."

"Thanks; I will."

I exited the dorms and went looking for Lombardo. It was easy to see him in the parking lot as he towered over everyone and everything.

"How'd it go with the roommate?" he asked.

"Better than you thought. It turns out Katrina met someone at a club the week before she took the bus home."

"And?"

"The roommate doesn't recall much about him or if Katrina heard from him again. She did tell me her roommate wasn't one to talk to anyone random unless it was in a social setting, wouldn't talk to anyone on the bus, and wouldn't go home with someone she just met."

"So, you basically found out nothing useful."

"What the hell? That just gave us a lot about our victim."

"All you told me is she met someone at a club. There's nothing else to go on. We already knew she was on the bus. I got a video showing her on the bus. So unless you got the name of the guy she met or a description, you got nothing."

"The roommate never saw the guy, but at least we know where they met. We can get a warrant to get the security footage from that night and check to see who she talked to that night."

"You're wasting time." Lombardo opened the door to his Jeep, but I grabbed him by the elbow.

"What happened with your person?"

"Nothing you need to concern yourself with."

"Oh hell no. We're working this case together. I deserve to know."

He ripped his arm free from my grasp. "You don't deserve shit. This is my case. You're here to help me." He jumped in the driver's seat and slammed the door shut.

"Where are you going?"

"I got someplace I gotta be, kinda like you last night." He started the Jeep and sped off out of the parking lot. I was left feeling like a complete idiot. Lombardo knew about my meeting with Victor and he decided to use me to get additional info from the roommate. He must have learned something from the other girl and was now going off on his own. But that wasn't going to stop me; nothing would until I found Valentina.

Chapter 15-Ali

Another day gone, and Valentina and the other victims were still missing. I felt like such a failure. The poor girls should've been home with her parents, but yet she was still in the hands of some creepy men with villainous intentions. I wanted to do more, but didn't know how. I was at a loss, with no solid leads to work from.

Pulling into my driveway made me feel even worse. I was able to come home, take a hot shower, and climb into a nice comfy bed. I imagined Valentina and the other girls were sitting in some dark, dingy basement, shackled to a pole and starving. It was tough to think of them in such a horrific situation. Valentina was nearly the same age as my sister. Seeing Amanda's car in the driveway eased my fears.

"I'm home," I called out after opening the front door. A few steps in, I saw a figure sitting on the couch in the living room. It wasn't James; it wasn't anyone I recognized. I un-holstered my gun, pointing it at the mystery man. "Who the fuck are you, and why are you in my house?"

"You must be Ali," the man said as he began to stand.

"Sit your ass back down and don't move or I swear I will put a bullet in you." I watched the man take a seat on the couch in the same spot I found him in.

"Look, I'm not here to hurt you."

"Then why are you in my house?"

"I was invited."

Before I could ask who invited him, Amanda entered the room. She shrieked when she saw me pointing my gun at the man and rushed to his side.

"Ali, what the hell are you doing?"

"You know this man?"

She jumped in front of him as he slowly rose to his feet. "Of course I know him; he's my boyfriend." It took me by surprise. I was frozen to the spot with my gun ready to put a bullet in the skull of my sister's supposed boyfriend. "Ali," Amanda growled. "You mind putting the gun away?"

I shook the look of surprise off my face and holstered my weapon instantly. "I-I'm sorry. I wasn't expecting a guest."

"Really? You've been begging me for the last few days to bring Lucas by to meet you. I thought you would be jumping at the chance to interrogate him. Although the gun probably was a bit overkill."

I glared at Amanda. "Yes, I've been asking to meet your boyfriend and yes, my reaction might be considered overkill. But do you really blame me for how I reacted? After all we've been put through? Think about it from my point-of-view, Amanda." I took a deep, calming breath then returned my focus to the man standing in the living room wearing a tan suit. I had to admit, he had a much better appearance than the other guys Amanda dated. "You have to excuse me. It's been a bit crazy around here lately, and I wasn't really expecting company."

"It's okay. Your sister told me you were a cop. It was my mistake for coming over unexpectedly." He glanced back at Amanda before focusing on me. "Maybe we should do this another time."

I could feel the heat from Amanda's eyes staring me down. "No, wait…you don't have to go. Please, stay for a while."

"Good, maybe we can start over," Amanda suggested. "Preferably, without you pulling a gun on my boyfriend," she added quickly.

"I think that can be arranged…for now," I replied while my hand rested on the butt of my glock. I caught Amanda at the corner of my eye giving me a disapproving look.

Her boyfriend stuck out his hand. He stared at my hand before making eye contact with me. "I'm Lucas."

"Lucas, you got a last name?"

"Everette," he replied.

"Nice to meet you, Mr. Everette; I'm Detective Ryan."

"Ali," Amanda growled.

"But you can call me Ali." I shook Lucas's hand and released instantly. I didn't want to be accused of trying to intimidate the poor guy. "So, what do you two have planned for tonight?"

"We were planning on going to dinner soon," Amanda replied.

"Oh great; let me call James and find out when he'll be home, maybe we can double."

"That's not exactly what we had in mind, sis."

"It's fine, Amanda. I don't mind sharing you for a night. Besides, it would be nice to get to know your sister and her husband a little more."

"Oh, I'm not married. We're just dating."

"You've been dating long?"

"No, not really; maybe a few months."

"Well…if he's smart, he won't waste too much time before he puts a ring on that finger."

I guess I should've been flattered. I could only assume he meant it as a compliment. But the tone in his voice made me think he was flirting.

"Thanks, but I wouldn't want to impose on your dinner plans."

"Please, we insist."

"We do?" Amanda asked.

"Yes, of course."

"Okay," I said hesitantly. "Let me get changed and give James a call." I took a few steps backward out of the room. Lucas leaned in to whisper something to my sister, but his eyes were locked on me.

I walked down the hall and entered my room. I kicked off my heels and began peeling off my work clothes while dialing James's cell. Both times I tried, the call went to voicemail.

"Hey," he said on the final ring.

"And here I thought you were trying to ignore me."

"Ali, I can't really talk right now. What's up?"

"My sister brought her boyfriend over to meet us. We were going to double and go out to dinner with them."

"I can't tonight; I'm working."

"Okay, how much longer are you gonna be?"

"I…I don't know, babe. I can't really be on the phone right now."

"What should I do about my sister?"

"See if you can reschedule or go out to dinner with them."

"Are you gonna meet us at the restaurant?"

"Probably not; I'm up to my neck with this case."

"Then I guess I'll stay home."

"Just go with them. This is what you wanted anyway."

"Yeah, but I expected you to be there too."

"Well, I can't tonight. So you need to make the most of the opportunity and go out with them. You can tell me all about it later."

"Fine," I pouted. "But just so you know, you're missing out on me standing in our room in nothing but a pink thong."

"You better be wearing that when I get home tonight."

"Maybe, or maybe I won't be wearing anything at all."

"Baby, you're killing me."

"Then I guess you need to hurry up and come home."

"I promise I'll be there as soon as I can. I love you."

"You better." I smiled as I pulled on a pair of jeans. "See you soon, loverboy." I hung up and continued getting dressed before walking back to the living room. "Bad news; James is stuck at work."

"Bummer," Amanda said who was obviously faking her sympathy. She turned to Lucas and grabbed his hand. "I guess it's just us tonight."

"I guess so…I mean…unless your sister still wants to go."

"What?"

"No," I replied while shaking my head. "I wouldn't want to intrude. I'd be like the third wheel."

"Nonsense," Lucas replied. "I insist."

I glanced over at my sister whose face had turned bright red. I could tell she wasn't happy with either of us. I doubted she would let me have another chance to go near her boyfriend in fear of what I would say or do. Hell, I already pulled a gun on him.

"Sure, I'd love to go to dinner with you guys." I could almost hear the curses being muttered under Amanda's breath. If we lived in a cartoon world, she'd be beet red with a whistle blowing and steam coming out of her ears.

We walked out of the house in silence to Lucas's car. He was driving a white Lexus. He opened both the rear and passenger side doors and waited for us to enter before closing them. He drove us into Poughkeepsie and brought us to one of the hottest restaurants, Crave. He helped us from the car and opened the door for us as we entered the building.

Amanda picked a guy with manners and acted chivalrous? Maybe she finally grew up and decided to date the right kind of guy. I wanted to give my sister the benefit of the doubt, but only time would tell. I was a cop and could see through someone's bullshit. If this was some act Lucas was putting on to get my approval, I would figure it out by the end of dinner and call them out on it.

The waiter promptly greeted us at our table and took our drink orders. Lucas and Amanda ordered wine, but I decided to be the sober one and had a glass of water with lemon. We studied our menus for a couple of minutes while the waiter retrieved our drinks. The conversation lingered on what we wanted to eat. I decided on the roasted chicken breast. Amanda settled on the panisse, and Lucas ordered the Long Island duck.

Once we had placed our orders, I turned my attention to Amanda's boyfriend. "So, Lucas; tell me about yourself."

His eyes shifted to my sister momentarily before he straightened up in his chair. "Okay, Detective, what would you like to know about me?"

"Let's start with how you met my sister."

"We met a few months ago at a bar. She was out with her friends and I was with some co-workers. We found ourselves trying to order at the same time. I offered to buy her a drink and we kept talking for the rest of the night."

"Did anything happen between you two that night?"

"Ali," Amanda snapped. "That's none of your business."

Maybe it was, but to me it was an appropriate question. Amanda had been going through a rough patch after the murder of her boyfriend Shawn. I needed to make sure this guy wasn't preying on that and using her for sex since.

"Nothing happened other than the two of us exchanging numbers and an innocent kiss to end the night," Lucas replied.

Innocent my ass. I couldn't help but continue to question him, even after being so blunt and direct with the first one. "So what is your intention with my sister?"

"Ali," Amanda snapped again. I knew she was going to ream me out later for this, but I needed to know who she was dating and so did she.

"I'm not sure I follow," Lucas replied.

"Well, my sister was thinking of moving out and I wanted to know where you see this relationship going?"

"I care about Amanda very much."

"Do you love her?"

I saw the two of them glance at each other. I doubted either of them said those three words to the other yet. "Yes, I do," Lucas said in a matter of fact tone.

"Do you plan on marrying her?"

"Ali, that's enough." Amanda stood up from the table and was hovering over me. "Lucas, you don't have to answer that or any of her questions."

"I want to further explore my relationship with Amanda before making that decision. I feel marriage is a lasting commitment and you want to be sure the person you marry is the one you plan on spending the rest of your life with."

"Then why have her move in if you're not sure?"

"That's it," Amanda slammed her hands on the table. "We're done here. Ali, you can find your own way home. We're leaving."

Lucas grabbed Amanda by the hand and whispered something in her ear. He guided her back to the chair, but she refused to look at me. Her cheeks were flaring red hot as she stared a hole into the center of the table.

"As I stated, I love your sister. I want to be with her. By having her move in, we can get a glimpse into our future as a married couple and decide if this is what we really want."

I decided to back-off a bit and only asked one more simple question to get to know Lucas a little better. "What do you do for a living?"

"I work at an investment corporation, managing accounts and showing my clients the best ways to increase their earnings with different investment solutions."

Damn, this guy was good. He seemed to have the perfect answer for every question I threw at him. I didn't know whether to be impressed or to be more suspicious.

He grabbed Amanda's hand and whispered something into her ear again. The red in her cheeks faded into a more normal color for her. Her eyes flashed to me as she lifted her wine glass. She took a big sip as Lucas leaned back in his chair.

He released her hand and looked at me. His fingers pinched the stem of his glass as he swirled the wine around. He raised his hand slowly and winked at me as he brought the glass to his lips.

He winked at me...he fucking winked at me. Who the hell does that? Why the hell did he do it? The guy was winning me over with how nice and charming he was, and then he does something weird and creepy like wink at me.

From that moment on, I didn't want anything to do with Lucas. I sat silently in my chair, eating my dinner until it was time to go home. It was a quiet meal, but I wasn't that hungry, and by the looks of it, Amanda wasn't either. We both took our meals to-go as Lucas paid the bill.

"You didn't have to do that," I said. I would've paid for myself.

"Nonsense," he replied. "You were our guest. I was more than happy to take the two loveliest ladies in Ulster County out to dinner." He escorted us out to the car and held the doors open again. It was the most awkward night I ever had, and I had a feeling it would get worse when I got home.

Chapter 16-Ali

There was silence in the car throughout the whole drive back to my house. I could see Lucas's eyes shifting to steal a glance at Amanda before checking on me through the rearview mirror. I could tell he wanted to break the tension by saying something, but that would only be the spark to ignite the time-bomb that was my sister.

When he pulled up in front of the house, he reached for his seatbelt, but Amanda's hand stopped him. She was ending the nice chivalry act he had put on all night. I took the hint and gladly opened my own door.

"Thank you for dinner," I said as I exited the car into the cool night air. I walked up to the path and entered the empty house alone.

I kicked off my flats and entered the kitchen to grab a beer. I started downing the bottle as I heard the door slam shut.

Time for a war. I stepped into the living room to find Amanda staring me down as if she were ready to attack me.

"How fucking dare you?" she snarled.

"I know I may have step over the line a little-"

"A little? You went way over the line tonight. You had no right to ask those questions. We haven't even discussed any of those topics."

"And yet you wanna move in with this guy whom you've known all of a month maybe two?"

"I love him and he loves me; that's all that matters."

"But yet he didn't say those words until tonight."

"He didn't have to; I already knew."

"Bullshit, Amanda. You thought it, may have believed it, but you didn't know for sure until he said those three words to you tonight."

"Why is it any of your fucking business?"

"For starters, you're my sister."

"And that gives you carte blanche to know every little aspect of my life, who I date, and everything about their life too?"

"It does after everything we went through together. We just got one psycho out of our lives. That son of a bitch wreaked havoc on us. He stole our sanity, our sense of security, and our loved ones. I wanna make sure we don't let someone else like that near us again."

"That was your fault, not mine. You were the one who worked with the psycho. You were the one he wanted revenge against. I lost the man I loved as collateral damage. And I was the one being used as bait to get to you."

"Don't you dare put this on me. I didn't invite him into our lives."

"But you didn't do a damn thing to keep him away from us either."

"No, I just kept putting myself out there to find the psycho. I was the one who risked my life time and time again to draw him out. It was partially my plan that took him down."

Amanda clapped slowly. "Bravo," she said slowly. "Do you want a medal or something? Do you need another headline calling you a hero?"

"What the hell is that supposed to mean?"

"It means I'm sick of hearing how great you are, or how heroic you were in taking down three psychopathic killers. I'm sick of people hearing my name and associating it with you. I want to be my own person. I want a life of my own away from you and this fucked up life."

"So, you're using Lucas just so you can get away from me?"

"No, I love that man. But I need my own life and I can't do that being around you. He had a spare room at his place and offered it to me. Yes, we would be living together, but it would be to help me find myself and to see what a life together could be."

I was stunned and hurt by her comments. I didn't know Amanda felt that way. Maybe I was too consumed with hunting the killers to notice how it affected her.

I opened my mouth to respond, but heard the door slam against the wall. I ran to the edge of the living room to see James stumbling through.

"What the hell? James, are you okay?"

"Heeyyyyyy, baby," he slurred.

"Are you drunk?"

"Yes, but don't be mad."

Mad? He thought I'd be mad. Why? Because it was almost ten o'clock and he came home piss ass drunk when he should've been out on the double date with us? Yeah, I think I had every right to be mad.

I looked behind me to see the empty space where Amanda was standing. "You mind telling my why you're drunk off your ass or how you got home?"

He put his hand on my shoulder. "I can't go into detail; just know it's all part of the case I'm working on."

"Really? What kind of case requires you to get this drunk?"

"I can't go into detail right now, but it is part of my undercover work for the case."

"Then at least tell me how you got home." I peered out the window to see his car missing from the driveway. Lucas was still sitting in the street which meant Amanda was still in the house.

"I don't really wanna say."

"Why?" I asked. Okay, maybe I demanded.

"Because I know you're gonna be pissed."

"You better fucking tell me, James. I'm not in the mood for games tonight." I had a feeling about who drove him home and wasn't happy about it. The fact he was trying to hide it made things worse.

"I shared a cab with Jocelyn. We dropped her off first before I came back here." He wouldn't look me in the eyes. He had to have known I would be pissed off once he told me the truth.

"And tell me; how long ago *did* you drop her off, James?"

"Fifteen or twenty minutes ago." He looked down at his watch and saw the time. "Fuck, maybe like a half hour or forty minutes tops; I swear."

"So let me get this straight, you went out somewhere with your ex-girlfriend, got shit-faced drunk and took her home."

"Nothing happened, Ali; I promise."

I heard the front door slam and I knew it was Amanda running out to get as far away from me as she could. I checked the window and saw her jump in the passenger seat as Lucas drove away.

I turned back to James. "You better tell me the truth and don't leave out any details. I wanna know exactly what happened tonight."

"I've been working undercover at a financial investment company. We believe they've been conning their clients into putting their money into bullshit companies and investments."

"I already know this, James. I want to know about tonight."

"I've been trying to get close to one of the bosses and was asked to meet him for a business dinner tonight and to bring Jocelyn along. We were talking about working with some of his clients. I don't know how, but I lost track of how many I had and got really drunk. He paid for dinner and had the place call us a cab. We gave Jocelyn's address first and dropped her off. I walked her to the door; that's it, nothing else happened."

He took a step towards me, holding out his hands. But I didn't want to hear it after the night I had and kept him at an arm's distance. "And I'm supposed to believe your bullshit?"

"You're supposed to believe in me," he replied calmly.

"You're so lucky I love you, jerk."

"Hey, it's a step up from being called an asshole all the time. Now, you mind telling me what I stumbled into tonight?"

"You mean besides the front door?" We shared a light-hearted laugh before I turned to look back at the spot where Lucas's car was on the street. "Let's just say it was another blow up with my sister, and this time I think I may have overstepped a bit."

"A bit?"

"Okay…a lot. But I was looking out for her best interest."

"I'm sure you were, babe." James took a chair from the kitchen and sat down. "You have to remember something; your sister is an adult and can make her own choices. You need to trust her. If she makes a bad decision, it's on her to fix it; not you."

I walked over to James and put my arms around his neck. "I know, but she's my little sister. I'm the only family she has here."

"And if she needs advice or help, she'll ask for it. You gotta let her grow up and be her own person."

"Yeah, she pretty much said the same thing tonight. I think she's serious about moving out."

"Then you need to relax and let Amanda worry about herself. Who knows; maybe when she moves out we can finally learn to have fun again."

"Who says we need her to move out to have some fun?" I straddled James and ran my fingers through his hair. I could feel his hands caress my back as he buried his face against my chest.

"Baby, I think we need to take this to the bedroom before I lose my mind," he whispered.

His lips left a trail of scorching hot kisses along the base of my neck.

"No, I want you right here." I unbuttoned his shirt and let my fingers trace the muscles on his chest. I started grinding away, feeling him getting harder with every passing second.

"The curtains are still open."

"So, we can close them," I said as I traced his tattoos.

"What if your sister comes home?"

"Somehow I doubt she's coming back tonight." I grabbed a fistful of James's hair and pulled him towards me. I kissed him harder than I ever had before and felt the passion reciprocated.

I couldn't explain what came over me. I just knew I needed him more than ever in that moment. I needed to feel his arms around me. I continued kissing the side of his neck. Then the innocent little kisses turned into nibbles, which turned into more.

"Ow," he said with a flinch. "What the hell?"

"What; you never got a hickey before?"

"No, I usually gave them."

"Well then, I guess it's time I left my mark on you." I continued sucking on his neck as he started to thrust into me.

"You better go close those curtains before we give the neighbors a show they'll never forget."

"Fine. I'll be right back."

I strutted to the other side of the living room, shaking my ass in my tight pants with every step I took. I leaned towards the window and managed to grab the curtains before feeling James' hands around my waist. He wasted no time yanking my pants down with my panties. I didn't know what to do. The window was high enough not to show my bottom half, yet a part of me was excited to see what he would do next.

He dropped to the couch and lowered himself beneath me. His hands groped my ass, pulling me down. I could feel his hot breath on my skin as his tongue snaked out and found its way to my clit.

"James," I gasped.

He ignored me and continued on. I had to let go of the curtains before I ripped them off the wall. I'm sure knocking myself out while my boyfriend goes down on me would be super sexy.

I dug my nails into the top of the couch as James devoured me. He knew just the right spots to hit to make my toes curl. It didn't take long for him to bring me to the edge. I knew I was about to cum and would do so in front of an open window. But something about it turned me on and I wanted more.

"Oh fuck!" I shouted as I felt the much needed release. James slipped out from under me and smiled. "Oh my god, James; that was amazing."

"Well, I'm not done yet." He grabbed my waist and brought me back to a standing position. I heard a smack and a stinging sensation on my ass.

"Oh no," I protested. "Not out here."

"Come on; no one's watching."

I heard the sound of him unzipping his pants and then his belt hitting the floor. He was serious about giving the neighbors a show. I could feel how hard he was as he teased my pussy with the tip. I wanted to say no, but again, it was something that secretly turned me on.

He waited to hear if I would protest again, but he never heard those words escape my mouth. After a minute of teasing, he entered slowly so it wouldn't be a complete shock. He picked up speed gradually until I was gripping the top of the couch for support again.

"Harder," I gasped. There was no need to tell him twice. He had a plan and was executing it perfectly. Another smack across my ass made him thrust faster until I was begging for more. He reached forward and wrapped his fist in my hair, giving it a slight tug while spanking me again.

I couldn't take much more. I lost track of time and how many times I had cum. When he finished, I collapsed onto the couch in front of him. My legs were like Jell-o and weren't working. He curled up next to me on the couch and kissed me gently before scooping me into his arms to bring me to bed.

Chapter 17-HT

Javier spent the morning sleeping off the previous night. He was content with staying in bed all day. He wasn't due to be back at work until the next day. By seven that night, he received a knock on his door causing him to drag himself to his feet.

Javier opened the door, finding Dimitri standing outside. "What the hell are you doing here?"

"To get you." He pushed his way inside the apartment and headed towards the bedroom. "Come on; the boss wants us to pick up the girls from last night."

"He didn't say anything about grabbing them tonight."

"That's because he told me."

"When?"

"I couldn't help but tell him all about last night. Once he realized how much of a freak those two girls were, he didn't think twice about giving me the order."

Javier tried to remember the night with the girls, but everything was fuzzy after they had left the bar. The last thing he remembered was being helped into the back of the van.

"What happened-did you drug me last night?"

"You needed to loosen up. I thought you'd take advantage of it, but you just laid there like a dying dog. But don't worry; I took both girls out for a test drive, and man they didn't disappoint."

Javier grabbed Dimitri by the shirt and slammed him against the wall as hard as he could. "You ever pull that shit again, or put anything in my drink again, I will end you."

"Chill the fuck out," Dimitri replied while pushing Javier back. "I needed you to relax and have some fun, instead of pining over some bitch that's gonna be used and abused by every guy here."

Javier got in his face again. "No one touches her; you got it?"

"Yeah, I got it, and I'll help you make sure no one else does as long as you get your head on straight. Are you in?"

"Yeah, I'm in. Where are we meeting them?"

"I had someone following the girls all day. They're going to some frat party in New Paltz tonight. I figure we casually run into them, party together for a while, maybe have some after-party fun, and bring them back here."

"Fine, give me two hours to get ready and we'll go."

Javier shoved Dimitri out the door and stormed back into his bedroom. Anger consumed his every thought. He was furious over Dimitri giving him the assignment, even angrier at the boss for not telling him first. Javier felt a level of uneasiness. He was always the boss's right hand man, and now he was being given his orders by someone else. He needed to check with the boss and ensure the information he received was correct. He grabbed his cell and attempted to place the call, finding his phone had been powered off.

"Well, that makes more sense," he mumbled to himself as he turned the device on. Javier jumped in the shower as he waited for the phone to power on. As he shut off the water and looked down at his cell, he noticed a voicemail.

"Javi," the boss's voice boomed over the speaker. "Dimitri told me all about those two girls you snagged last night. It sounds like they are perfect for us. I want you both to bring them in tonight."

Javier put down the phone and became more relaxed as he searched for something to wear. Most of his clothes were too nice or were meant to go out to a club. But Dimitri told him they were going to a frat party and needed to dress the part so he didn't stick out.

As he dressed, Javier started to think about the girls they met at the bar and how much fun he had before Dimitri drugged everyone. It made him think about the future again, and how badly he wanted to share his life with someone. But the life he lived was not one meant to be shared with another person, and the woman he wanted to be with would eventually be sold to some rich pompous asshole. He remembered how Dimitri acted the other night and thought about seeing Valentina drugged up and being led away by some bastard that would use and abuse her.

Javier could feel the bile in his throat. He made a mad dash to the bathroom, making it to the toilet just in time. He hated thinking about Valentina's future. In that moment, Javier decided he needed to do something for her, even if it meant he had to buy her himself.

"Yo, open up," Dimitri yelled as he slammed a fist on the door.

"What the fuck is your problem?" Javier snarled as he greeted him.

"We need to go."

"What's the rush? The party will probably start by the time we get there. No one shows up that early."

"I just wanna find those two and..." he let out a smirk that told Javier what Dimitri's plans were for the night.

"Let me guess; you wanna fuck them again before bringing them in?"

"Hell yeah I do."

"Do what you want; just leave me out of it."

"So I can have them both?"

"You have my blessing. Now, get going before I change my mind."

The two left the complex and drove out to New Paltz. The town seemed quieter than usual. The bars didn't have as many people waiting outside to get in, and there weren't many people walking along

Main Street. The van took a quick turn and double-backed driving along the back roads until they found the frat house.

The block was lined with cars leading up to the party, while dozens of students marched in small groups destined to appear at the same location.

Dimitri left the van parked near the end of the block. It was their usual plan; keep the van out of sight and walk the drugged and drunk women away until they were able to load them into the back without anyone noticing.

They walked up the block and paid the ten dollar fee to get into the party. "Kegs are in the back; dollar shots in the kitchen," the man at the door said.

The goal was simple; get in, find the girls, drug them, and get out without anyone noticing they were missing. The moment they entered the house, Javier watched Dimitri split off to search his way, by hitting on every girl he met. There was one in particular that he kept circling. She was a skinny pale girl with hair as black as coal. She looked strangely familiar, but couldn't place where he knew her. He waited to see Dimitri strike out before motioning to follow him outside.

"You find them?" Dimitri asked while filling up his cup.

"No sign of the girls. What about you?"

"Nothing, but I saw a lot of chicks that would be perfect to satisfy me for a few hours."

"Yeah well, we're not here for that tonight. We need to find those two and bring them in. That's the plan."

"Fine, as long as I get one more round with each chick."

Javier rolled his eyes as he took a sip of from his cup. He turned around and saw another small group of girls hanging out in the backyard. He tapped Dimitri on the shoulder and pointed out the two from the bar.

"I think tonight got a whole lot easier."

Dimitri grabbed two more cups and filled them with beer. Javier caught him slipping something into each drink before one was pushed into his hands.

"Follow my lead." The two men walked down the deck steps and towards the group. Dimitri put his arm around Sandy's shoulder. "Hey gorgeous; I didn't think I'd be seeing you tonight."

The woman stared at him for a moment as Javier stood next to Brenda. She smiled and melted into his arm. "If I didn't know any better, I'd say you were following us," she laughed, not realizing the truth behind her statement.

"How about you two lovely ladies join us for a drink and pickup where we left off last night?"

Sandy grabbed the cup from Dimitri and chugged it down. "Sure, but there's no pool table here tonight. How are you gonna show me how to work the stick?"

"Oh, I'm sure we can find other ways to show you how to handle my stick." He directed Sandy away from the group, leaving Javier and Brenda behind.

"Are you gonna feed me the same bullshit line?" Brenda asked.

"No. But you're more than welcome to hang out with me and have some fun while those two do their thing."

Brenda took the cup from Javier as she excused herself from her friends. They looked at them suspiciously, but neither cared enough to follow their friend.

Javier walked with Brenda around the yard. Going inside the house would make it more difficult to talk over the loud music, and would increase the likelihood of losing her in the sea of drunken idiots.

"So, what happened last night?" Brenda asked.

Starting the conversation off with the missing pieces of a night out with two strangers was not part of the plan. "What do you mean?"

"I mean you got pretty shit faced, then I guess I did too. I remember all of us stumbling out of the bar, and then waking up in my bed. Everything else was a bit of a blur."

"Honestly, I don't remember anything after the bar. I think I mixed way too much last night and blacked out. I woke up in the back of my buddy's car in a puddle of drool; at least I hope it was drool."

"Ew," she replied with a bit of laughter in her voice. "So tell me; are we bound to have a repeat of last night?"

"No, I promise it won't be like last night."

"So then what are you doing at a frat party?"

"My friend dragged me here and told me he needed his wingman."

Brenda looked over her shoulder and around the yard. "Funny, it doesn't look like he needed one."

"I don't think he was expecting to run into you and Sandy tonight."

"I don't think either of us expected to hear from you guys again after last night. I mean, we didn't exchange numbers or anything."

"Did you want my number?" Javier said smoothly.

"Maybe. It depends on what you're looking to get out of this tonight."

"What if I want to get to know you more and see where things go?"

"Then, I'd probably say you were full of shit. No one comes to a frat party looking to get to know someone."

"So, if I told you I wanted to get you drunk so I could fuck the shit out of you, would that be more believable?"

"That's what every guy here is looking to do. Why should you be any different? I mean, look at how we met."

Javier downed his drink and held out his hand. "Then come with me and I'll prove you wrong."

Brenda finished what was left in her cup and grasped Javier's hand. They exited through a side gate and walked down the block.

"So tell me; what's your major?" he asked.

"I'm going to school to be a teacher."

"Elementary or high school?"

"I'm thinking elementary school. I love little kids and think it would be great to help them learn what they need to in life."

Javier stood back and admired the woman before him. He thought she was different than the rest of the girls he abducted and was already having second thoughts about sticking to the plan.

"So you like kids, you wanna make a difference in the world; what else can you tell me about yourself?"

He could see Brenda's eyes getting heavy. She took a step and stumbled into Javier's arms. "I-I like to watch movies," she slurred. Brenda leaned on Javier as he helped her stand. "I-I promise; I didn't have that much to drink tonight."

"I believe you," he whispered as they continued down the block.

"You must think I'm a drunk. I really don't drink a lot."

"It's okay. I'll get you to the car and take you back to the dorms. You can sleep it off and we can talk more tomorrow."

Brenda's legs started to give out by the time they reached the white van at the end of the block. Javier really did want to bring her back to the dorms and scrap the plan, but that option was gone the moment he saw Dimitri laying Sandy in the back of the van.

"Good, you're here," Dimitri said. He rushed over and helped place Brenda next to her unconscious friend. "Get in and let's go before someone sees us."

Javier wanted to say no. He wanted to stop everything from happening, but he knew if he purposely screwed up, the boss would kill him.

Dimitri drove back to the complex but stopped at a motel two miles away. "What are you doing?" Javier asked.

"I told you I wanted a piece of them again before we drop them off."

"You really think it's a good idea to bring them here after we just kidnapped them? If anyone sees them, we're fucked and could lead the cops back to the complex."

"You're a fucking buzzkill; you know that?"

"Whatever; I just don't feel like being thrown in jail or having a bullet between my eyes."

Dimitri put the van in drive and pulled out of the parking lot. "You're such a fucking pussy. Try taking some risks every once in a while and enjoy life for a bit."

"Yeah, I'll be sure to take your advice."

They made their way back to the complex and brought the girls into the area where they kept everyone. Dimitri took Sandy to his place first, no doubt to make good on his word from earlier. Javier didn't bat an eye or protest. It was Dimitri's decision to make and would need to deal with whatever consequences came as a result.

Javier carefully scooped up Brenda into his arms and carried her inside. He removed her personal items; purse, wallet, earrings, and necklace. Then he took her to the room and gently placed her on an empty bed. Her hands were chained to the wall above her head as she slept peacefully.

"I'm sorry," he whispered as he kissed her forehead.

He started to walk out of the room when he heard a woman moaning on the opposite side of the room. He knew the sound. Someone was desperate for another fix and had been too long since their last hit. He inched closer to the one making all the noise and noticed it was Valentina.

"Please, I need more," she cried in a whisper.

"I'll let the guard on duty know."

"No, please...I'll do anything. I need it now."

Javier wanted to hear those words so badly. He wanted to be the one to break Valentina and take her before all the others, but he couldn't bring himself to do it.

"I'll get you a fix, but it won't be as much as you usually get."

"Why? I need it. Please, I'll do anything. I'll suck you off. I'll let you do whatever to me. You can take my virginity. I don't care."

"Virginity," Javier said as he jumped back. That was something he didn't know about Valentina. Stealing someone's virginity was something he wouldn't do. It wasn't something that should be forcefully taken or sold to someone. He knelt down on the bed. "You need to trust me. I'm gonna help you. I don't know how, but I'll find a way to get you out."

Javier quickly left the room and returned minutes later with a syringe filled up less than it usually was. He injected Valentina with it and watched her face relax. He brushed the strands of hair from her face and wiped the sweat from her forehead.

"I promise; I'll find a way to get you out of here."

Chapter 18-Ali

The next morning I woke up just in time to see James leaving for work. He was dressed in a suit. It was the most dressed up I ever saw him, but I guess he had to play the part while undercover. I understood he had to get to the station before driving to job, but I still wished we had a little time together in the morning.

I had the morning to myself. It was the first day I didn't have to drive to the airport to meet with Lombardo at the Port Authority office outside JFK Airport. I needed to check-in to report any findings or to see if they needed me, but I had something else in mind to start my day.

I got dressed and headed for the station. It had only been a few days, but it felt like forever since I had been there. I was walking in with a purpose, and that was to rid myself of Eric Lombardo.

A few heads turned to stare as I entered the station. They didn't matter to me. I was focused and determined. I knocked on the lieutenant's door and walked in without giving him a chance to answer.

"Ryan, what are you doing here?" the lieutenant asked. I hadn't seen him in days, but he looked like shit. His hair was a mess, he wasn't wearing his jacket or tie, and his shirt looked like he slept in it.

"We need to talk."

"What is it? Did you find her?"

"Uh...no, sorry, sir."

"Then what is it?"

"I need to talk to you about Lombardo. I need you to talk to the captain and have him removed from the case."

"Why?"

"He's getting in the way. He's focused solely on the other missing girls, and isn't sharing information with me."

"Ali, this is between you and him; work it out."

"Yeah but, Lieu-"

"But nothing. He was working this case before you were. You were added as a favor to me because my daughter was missing. If you can't get along with your partner, then that's tough shit."

"How am I supposed to work with him when he's not sharing information from a missing girl's roommate?"

"That's between you two. I can't get involved. If I go to the captain with this, he'll take you off the case, not Lombardo."

"So you mean to tell me I'm stuck with him?"

"Unfortunately, you have no other choice."

"Thanks, Lieu." If he couldn't help me, then maybe it was time I gave my new partner a taste of his own medicine.

I stormed out of the station with the intent of conducting the investigation on my own. Instead, I walked right into the six-foot-two jackass I was trying to get away from.

"What are you doing here, Ryan?" he asked. "You trying to steal someone else's case?"

"Fuck you, Lombardo. I wanted to see how the lieutenant was doing."

"Yeah, sure you were," he mumbled.

"What the hell is that supposed to mean?"

"It means; you're a conniving little bitch who does whatever to get what she wants no matter who she hurts."

"Who did I hurt?"

"For starters, you turned your back on Rodney when he was a suspect in your boyfriend's murder."

"I was devastated and he was caught in the room standing over him with a gun in his hand. What the hell was I supposed to think at the time?"

"You should've trusted your partner."

"And I apologized for it; he forgave me; we got over it. I don't see how it has anything to do with you."

"He was my friend and partner before you came along. Then you get lucky with a case and got promoted. Next thing I knew they were re-assigning him to you because Esposito wanted to protect his new superstar."

"I get it now," I said. "You think if he was still your partner, you would've been assigned the Campus Killer case and all this crap notoriety would belong to you."

He tried to brush it off as if I was spinning some wild story that was far from the truth. His face had turned red and he refused to look me in the eyes. His hand reached into his pocket and pulled out his cell.

"You keep thinking that if it makes you feel better." He looked down at the phone again. "I gotta take this."

I glanced at the cell and didn't see anyone calling. I didn't hear a ringtone or it vibrating. "Bullshit. You're using it as an excuse."

"I don't need an excuse. I'm done with you."

Before I could respond, the station door slammed open. The lieutenant was standing behind us with flaring nostrils and fire in his eyes.

"You two, in my office, *now*," he snarled.

We were like two scolded dogs. We followed behind the lieutenant with our tails tucked firmly between our legs as we walked through the station back to his office. I could tell the other officers were staring at us. I could only assume they heard the argument. I mean; it wasn't like we were quiet about it or anything.

As soon as we entered his office, the lieutenant forcefully closed the door. "I've had it with you two."

"But, Lieu-" we both said in unison.

"Save it. I'm done listening to your bullshit. Lombardo, I know you have issues with her. I hear you talking shit behind her back to the other officers. But the fact remains; she's a damn good cop and probably the best one we got. She's on this case as a favor to me and to help you close a big case."

I started to smile. The words *suck it, bitch* came to mind. But the lieutenant must have read my mind and turned his attention to me.

"Wipe that smirk off your face, Ryan. I'm sick of you too."

"Me? What did I do?"

"I'm sick of your complaining, your need to always be right, and your arrogance of thinking you're smarter than everyone else."

"I wouldn't be complaining if I had a partner that actually worked with me and not someone who's trying to use this to advance his career."

"How haven't I worked with you?" Lombardo asked.

"You refused to share what the other roommate said during the interview the other morning."

"That's because there was nothing to tell. She wasn't in her room."

"Then why didn't you tell me?"

"Because it was fun to watch you squirm. The great Ali Ryan didn't get what she wanted for once and you blew up about it."

"That's what I'm talking about, Lieu. He'd rather play games than actually work together to solve this case."

"Oh, you mean how your buddy gave you a lead and instead of sharing it with your partner, you went off on your own to check it out and never said anything to me."

The lieutenant slammed his hands on the desk, causing us to jump back in our chairs. "Do you not understand what your bickering is doing? You are putting my daughter's life and the lives of the other missing girls at risk because you two can't put aside your differences. These girls are in hell right now and their only hope to get out of this alive are you two assholes. Now, can you work together for the sake of saving these girls?"

"I can as long as he's done playing games."

Lombardo glanced over at me with hatred in his eyes. "Fine, as long as she remembers we're a team."

I held out my hand with a fake smile on my face. "Deal."

He reluctantly accepted my gesture as the lieutenant rolled his eyes at us. "Good. Now, get the hell out of here and find those girls."

We exited the office and remained silent as we walked through the station. We were almost at the door when I heard Rodney yelling for us to come back.

"I just got a call from campus. Two girls were just reported missing after going to a party last night."

"Maybe they got laid and didn't come back yet," Lombardo quipped.

"Or maybe they were the next abduction victims," I replied. "Did the caller tell you anything else?"

"Just that their friends were approached by two men who seemed to know the girls."

I turned to Lombardo. "We need to look into this."

"You really think these guys are going to some college party to kidnap a couple of girls while their friends are nearby?"

"I can interview them alone, but I think it's better if we work as a team like you said."

"Fine," he replied while sighing. "Give us the info and we'll look into it." Lombardo grabbed the paper from Rodney and headed for the door with me close behind.

"I'm driving," I called out to him as we exited the building.

"Oh hell no. I've heard how dangerous you are behind the wheel. I'd like to get home tonight in one piece."

Chapter 19-Ali

I decided to let Lombardo have his way and had him drive to campus. It was my way of showing him I was willing to work as a team. Rodney advised there were two girls we needed to speak to and gave us the room number of the dorm they were staying in.

"You really think these girls were abducted?" Lombardo asked.

"Ask me that again after we talk to the friends. It could be nothing. They could've hooked up with a couple of guys and didn't come back to the dorms yet." I saw the gleam in his eyes at the mere thought of being right. "But I'd rather work under the assumption they're actually missing in case they really were kidnapped."

"Fine, but if I'm right, you owe me and the rest of the boys a round at the bar." I knew the one he meant. It was the same one all the cops in the area hit up after their shifts were over. It was the typical "boys club".

If I lost the bet, he was going to make me pay by emptying my wallet for every cop in Ulster County. I figured I would hurt him in a different way. "Okay, but if they really are missing, you owe me a drink at a bar of my choosing."

"Deal," he replied while extending his hand. I accepted without hesitation as he pulled up to the stop light to make a left.

We drove down the road and turned onto campus. Lombardo wasn't as familiar with navigating the area, so I offered to show him where to go. I hated being on the campus. I was always there for a case; whether it was showing up to a crime scene or to question some of the students.

We parked near the resident's lot and walked up to the dorm. We showed our badges and headed up to the second floor. The door flew open seconds after Lombardo knocked. Inside the room were two twenty year old girls who had hopeful looks on their faces only to have the crushing realization we weren't their missing friends.

"Is Tatiana here?" I asked. The girl nodded her head, causing me to assume the girl I was looking for was her. "I'm Detective Ryan, and this is my partner Detective Lombardo. As I understand, you called in a missing persons report about two of your friends."

"Their names are Brenda Blanchard and Sandy Michaels," Tatiana replied. "They met up with some guys last night and no one's heard from them since."

"Told you," Lombardo muttered under his breath.

I shot him a nasty look which he noticed and decided to take a few steps towards the door. "Where did they meet up with these guys?"

"We were all hanging out at some frat party off-campus. We were there for maybe a half hour before two guys showed up and steered them away from us."

"Do you know what these men looked like?"

"No," the other girl, Tessa, whimpered. "We were hanging out in the backyard. The only lights were on the back of the house which left the rest of the yard too dark to notice."

"Did they say anything or do anything suspicious when they approached your friends?" I asked.

"They each had two cups in their hands and gave one to Brenda and the other to Sandy." I did my best to hide the smirk that threatened to reveal itself at Tatiana's story. It wasn't much, but it was enough to prove something happened to the two girls during the party.

"Do you remember what time your friends walked off with the two men?" I was hoping to find some sort of time stamp I can put on the last time they were seen.

The girls conversed and thumbed through their phones. "We left for the party around ten," Tatiana said.

"We probably got there around ten-thirty," the other girl replied.

"I think they left us around eleven-twenty or eleven-thirty." The tone in Tatiana's voice made it sound more like a question than a statement.

I glanced back at Lombardo. "Do you have any questions?"

He cleared his throat and approached the girls. "Did Brenda or Sandy ever go home with guys they just met?"

"No," Tatiana replied quickly.

"Well," Tess said while her word lingered. "Brenda wasn't really into the partying crowd. Up until recently, she was in a relationship. Most of the time, she was the mom of the group and barely drank."

"And Sandy?" Lombardo asked.

"She was more of the party girl."

"Has she ever gone home with a guy before?"

"Yes, but it was always someone she knew. Sandy didn't hook up with random guys she just met. She usually conned them into buying drinks, make out with them a bit, and maybe exchange numbers by the end of the night."

"Did either Brenda or Sandy indicate they knew either of the guys from the party?"

"They definitely knew them, but I never met them before," Tatiana stated in a matter of fact tone.

"Did they talk about meeting someone recently?" I interrupted.

"Not that I know of," Tatiana replied.

"Sandy mentioned something to me yesterday," Tess confessed. "She told me not to say anything, but her and Brenda met two guys at a bar the other night."

"Did she say which bar or what happened?" I questioned.

"No. She actually couldn't remember much about the night or how she got back to her room. She told me the last thing she remembered was flirting with one of them while they played pool."

It was getting harder to contain my excitement. Tess was giving us several possible leads to work from which could've been the break in the case we needed.

"Do you have any further questions, Detective?" I asked.

"One more," he replied. "Where was this party last night?"

The girls gave us the address and walked us out of the room. "You know what this means? We've got some bar hopping to do, Lombardo."

He rolled his eyes and let out a deep sigh. "Fine, but let's check out this house where the party was last night. Maybe we can find something useful or someone that remembers seeing our suspects."

We drove to the edge of campus and parked in front of a familiar house. I stopped as we walked up the lawn, remembering the last time I stepped foot inside it.

"What's the matter?" Lombardo asked.

"I've been here before."

"What? You attended frat parties?"

"In another life…yes, but not here. This was the house Rachel Walker was at the night she was murdered."

"Oh," he mumbled. Yeah, his sarcastic, pig-headed remarks couldn't shake the memories that house stirred up.

I took a deep breath and stormed up the steps and wrapped my knuckles on the screen door. A young man with a short, spiky haircut answered.

"Can I help you?" he asked.

We showed him our badges and asked if we could come inside. He looked a bit nervous and called for his frat brother, Phillip. Moments later, a tall skinny African American male with a thin mustache appeared.

He took one look at me and shook his head. "No, not you," he cried out. "Whatever it is, we didn't do it."

"So you didn't have a huge party here last night?"

We glanced around the yard and inside the house. There were red cups littering the floor and the grass. They were even hidden in the bushes. There was no use denying the party happened.

"Look, kid," Lombardo interrupted. "We're not here to bust you for underage drinking, or for selling liquor or beer without a license to distribute. We just need to ask a few questions about a couple of girls that were here last night."

There was a sign of relief on Phillip's face, but then his eyes shifted to me. "Please tell me no one died."

"Not that we know of," Lombardo replied. "But both girls are missing, and we were hoping you and your frat brothers might be able to help us."

"Hey, we're always happy to help the police whenever we can." I could tell he was laying it on thick hoping we would stay away from him and his parties in the future. The fact one girl was murdered the year before and two more went missing less than twenty-four hours prior to our arrival, ensured I would be keeping a closer eye on Phillip and his frat brothers.

We entered the house, finding the living room was worse than I saw from the doorway. A table was knocked over, large black trash bags lined the wall, and more red cups covered the furniture.

"Here, have a seat," Phillip said as he quickly cleared the couch of any remnants from the party. "So how can I help you fine officers?"

I pulled up the pictures of the girls from my phone and showed them to Phillip. "Do you remember seeing either of them last night?"

"Not really, but then again I was working until eleven and didn't get back here until about midnight."

That wasn't going to help us. According to the friends, Brenda and Sandy were already with the mystery men and had been given something to drink. My gut told me they were laced with some sort of date rape drug to get the girls away from the party quickly.

"Can you grab the other frat brothers and ask them to talk to us for a bit?" Lombardo asked. "We're hoping one of them might remember these two and who they were with last night."

"Yeah, sure thing." Phillip searched the house and brought the members of his fraternity to meet us.

One-by-one we interviewed the young men who were still hungover from what appeared to be a hell of a party. None of them recalled seeing Brenda or Sandy, which didn't surprise me. Based on what their friends said, I didn't think they stayed long. Most of the brothers recited how many beers they had and how many chicks they made out with during the party, but couldn't give details about what anyone looked like. The hour and a half we spent at the house became a giant time suck. We weren't getting any answers from the frat house, and I was getting sick of hearing them make lewd comments about me when they walked into the kitchen to hang out with the others once we were done questioning them.

We left the house and walked back to the car with Lombardo grinning from ear-to-ear. "What the hell is so funny?" I asked.

"How much you wanna bet half of them make up some bullshit fantasy of you coming to the house about an investigation and slept with them instead."

"That's fucking gross."

"Yeah, but you know how frat boys are; they'll make up anything just to prove how much game they have to the other guys."

"Can we erase this part of the day from our memory and get back on track. We need to hit up the bars on Main Street to see if they recognize the girls."

"Fine by me. Besides, I think we need to get you a drink so you can loosen up a bit."

"Excuse me."

"Hey, I'm just sayin'; you always seem like you got something stuck up your ass." He looked over his shoulder quickly before snapping his attention back to me. "Maybe I shouldn't say that too loud. One of the frat boys might claim it was them."

"You're a disgusting piece of shit; you know that?"

"Come on; lighten up, Ryan."

"Just shut the fuck up and drive."

Chapter 20-HT

It should've been just another day for Javier. With every batch of girls, he monitored them in the mornings, and took them one-by-one to the basement. It was a dark, dingy, room smelling of sex. It was a playground of sorts for the men that worked for the boss. Men imposed their dominance over the women until they did as they were told.

Javier took his turns in the past, but mostly watched to make sure no one went too far. After all, he didn't want to report one of the guys messed up a piece of the boss' shipment. All of that changed the last few days. He found himself sitting in the security room, watching over the girls, especially Valentina.

She was sweaty and needed another hit. He was lowering the doses each time trying to wean her off slowly. He still didn't know how to save her. Javier wanted her for himself, but didn't want to force her to do anything she didn't truly desire.

He was about to grab another syringe from the safe when his cell started buzzing. He didn't need to look at the screen to know it was the boss. It was one of the few people who had his number.

"Hey, boss," Javier said.

"I need to see you in my office, now."

"Sure, I'll be right over."

Javier exited the security room and walked over to a smaller building. He knocked on the door and entered the room, finding the chair with its back to him.

"You wanted to see me?"

"You and Dimitri did good the other night. I think those two girls will make a fine addition to the collection."

"I'm glad you liked them."

"Yes…well…they were good, but not great. We need a few more before going to auction."

"Yeah, about that," Javier began. He didn't know where the courage to say something to the boss came from, but the words flowed easily from his mouth. "I was wondering if I could buy Valentina."

"Who?"

"The cop's daughter."

"You're joking; right? That girl could earn us a fortune."

"I'm not saying to give me her. I have plenty of money saved up."

"Oh really? How much are you willing to spend?"

"I have about a million stashed away and another two-hundred thousand in a bank account. Plus, you can use whatever you'd pay me for this shipment as part of my bid."

"I'll give it some thought and let you know soon enough. In the meantime, I need you to get the new girls ready and rush phase one. We need them ready and willing to comply in about a week."

"A week?"

The boss looked at Javier with a perplexed glare. "We need to move the girls fast and be on our way to the west coast. I want to put some distance between us and these asshole cops that are looking for your *girlfriend*." He laughed as he put emphasis on the term girlfriend.

"I can get them ready, boss."

"Good. I knew I could count on you. I suggest you begin A.S.A.P."

Javier turned to walk out of the room, when Dimitri entered, dragging a sweaty pale version of Valentina with him.

"Is she okay?" Javier asked.

"Nothing that a little medicine can't cure," Dimitri replied.

"I can run back and get her a dose."

"Nonsense," the boss said loudly. He opened his desk drawer and pulled out a black box. He filled the syringe to the full dosage and injected Valentina before Javier could utter another word of protest. They watched as Valentina regained her color and the sweating subsided. "There, that's better; isn't it, sweetheart?"

She nodded and kept quiet. Dimirti grabbed a handful of her hair and yanked her head back. "The boss asked you a question. I think he deserves a proper response."

"Yes," she meekly replied.

"Yes; what," Dimitri snapped.

"Yes, sir. Thank you."

Hearing Valentina utter those words crushed Javier. When he first saw her, he wanted to be her master, the man to break her. Seeing her succumb to the will of another man was devastating.

"Don't you have training to do?" the boss asked.

"Yes, but why is she here?" Javier knew what was about to happen. He had brought plenty of women to the boss' office and knew it was his turn to assess and rate the women according to his standards. Some were only asked questions, while others he took for a test drive.

"You should know by now how this works." He moved behind his desk and advised Valentina to sit in the chair across from him. "I'm going to ask you a set of questions. If you're a good girl and answer truthfully, you will be rewarded. If you lie or withhold an answer from us, Dimitri will have to discipline you. Do I make myself clear?"

"Yes, sir," she replied.

"Good. Let's start off with something simple. "When was the last time you had sex?" It was a simple question. Most girls tried to lie and say it's been a while or they fought and said it was none of their business.

Valentina was the opposite. She shrunk down in her chair with her cheeks turning a shade of bubble gum pink. It was unlike any response the men had seen.

Dimitri grabbed her hair and pulled her head back again. "Tell the boss what he wants to know," he snapped.

Javier shoved him back. "You think beating the answers out of her is going to get her to talk?"

"Both of you need to get a hold of yourselves, or you can get the fuck out of my office." The boss lowered himself back into his chair and focused on Valentina. "It's okay, sweetheart. It's nothing to be ashamed of; lots of people have sex."

"Not me," she whimpered.

"What do you mean; not you?"

Tears rolled down Valentina's cheeks. "I'm still a virgin." She sobbed silently as the boss rose out of his seat.

He approached Javier and clapped a hand onto his shoulder. "Sorry, my boy; her value just tripled. She's going to be the headlining piece of this shipment. She could easily go for twenty million or more."

"Better luck next time," Dimitri whispered with hatred in his tone.

"I tell you what," the boss said as he turned back towards his men. He had a smile on his face. "I'll do you one solid. You can watch as I finish prepping her for the auction, and you can use any other girl as your personal fuck toy."

Javier didn't want a fuck toy. He wanted something real and he wanted it with Valentina. He forced himself to sit through the interview, finding she was not entirely pure. She had messed around with a couple of guys at the end of high school and in college, but never lost her virginity.

Once the boss was satisfied with the answers to his questionnaire, he commanded Valentina to stand. It was the most humiliating part of the process.

"Strip down to your bra and panties," the boss demanded.

Valentina complied with his orders. She removed the black tank top first and then her jeans, showing off her curvaceous body. Dimitri grabbed a camera and snapped the pictures while the boss videotaped the whole humiliating ordeal.

"Remove your bra," he called out.

Dimitri moved in closer, making sure to get every angle possible. He adjusted the lens several times to zoom in and out. It was almost as if he was getting off on taking advantage of her and pissing off Javier.

"Now the panties."

More tears streaked down Valentina's face as she wrapped her thumbs in the fabric at her hips and regretfully pulled it down until she stood naked in front of three strangers.

Javier admired the beautiful sight in front of him, while the others acted like horny high school kids seeing their first pair of boobs. He waited until the men put down the cameras before turning his back to them. He heard Valentina take in a quick breath and sounded frightened. He spun back in time to see Dimitri licking two of his fingers.

"Sorry; I needed a little taste before we put that hot piece of ass up for sale." He shoved his fingers a little deeper inside his mouth and moaned. "Damn, she tastes good."

It took everything not to hit Dimitri. Javier's hand remained in a clenched fist, ready to attack, but he knew how it would look in front of the boss. He decided to keep his composure and distanced himself from Dimitri.

"Get the girl dressed and bring her back to the bed," the boss ordered.

Dimitri smiled as he made a move towards Valentina. Javier put a hand on him, pulling Dimitri back. "I'll take care of her. The boss wanted us to expedite the new girls and their training."

"Oh, that should be fun. I'll meet you down there."

Javier helped Valentina get dressed and walked her back to the room with the rest of the girls. He placed her gently on the bed before placing the cuffs on her wrists.

"You're such a liar," she snapped.

"What?"

"You said you were gonna help me. All you did was degrade me in front of those two pigs."

"I didn't do anything. I want to get you out of here, but we're running out of time."

"Bullshit."

"Hey, I offered to buy you and your freedom for more than a million dollars. I might've had a chance until you told them you were a virgin."

"You just wanted me to be your whore."

"As much as I would love to fuck the shit outta you, I'd rather see you happy and free from this place, even if your happiness wasn't with me."

"Liar."

"You'll see."

"Doubt it. Now just leave me alone."

"I'll never leave you, Valentina. I think I might love you."

"How can you say you love someone and hold them hostage to be sold to another man?"

Javier closed his eyes and took a deep breath. "I've never loved before. I don't think I have ever loved anyone. When I saw you for the first time, I knew I had to have you. It was primal at first, but the more I saw, the more I realized I wanted someone special in my life."

"And you think that's me?"

"I don't know…maybe. But I know I'll never figure that out while I'm here. That's why we need to make a break for it the first chance we have. I can take you with me out of the country. We can start our lives over somewhere new."

"Why would I ever go with you?"

"Because you would be in danger here. The boss would come after you just to get to me."

"You forget; my dad's the lieutenant."

"That didn't stop us from grabbing you in such a heavily guarded public place. We managed to pull off your kidnapping without a hitch. You don't think he could do it again?" He could see the wheels turning inside her head. "Please, just trust me. I will find a way to get us out of this mess; I promise."

Chapter 21-Ali

We pulled into a parking spot on Main Street which gave us the perfect view to most of the town's bars. We decided it was best to split up to cover more ground. It was obvious the kidnappers were still in the area, but we didn't know how much longer they were staying.

I didn't get much of a response from the employees at the bar. Most of them didn't work nights and didn't recognize either picture of the girls I showed them. I knew going during the day was a long shot, but it was the best chance to get someone to talk or to get a look at their surveillance cameras.

I knew the suspects didn't pick up the girls at the bar the night they went missing, and doubted they brought them out after leaving the party. My only hope was checking the footage the night before to see if we could find the girls. Maybe we would get lucky and find our two suspects following them or making a move on our most recent kidnapping victims.

Thankfully, the bar managers were happy to help and provided the footage without asking for a warrant. It made my day go by a lot faster and made it seem like it wasn't a waste of my time.

I walked back to the car when I was done and found Lombardo sulking in the driver's seat. "I'm guessing things didn't go quite like you planned," I said flatly.

"No one knew shit."

"Well duh, you're questioning the day crew about what happened during the night shift. How much did you really think you were gonna get out of them?"

"I figured someone might've worked late or switched shifts."

"Sounds like you were relying on dumb luck to give you the answers you wanted. Did you at least get their surveillance footage?"

"Yeah; did you?"

"Thankfully, we didn't need a warrant for them."

He sat in the driver's seat nodding his head. "You ready to go?"

"We have one more place to check out on the way back."

Lombardo pinched the sides of his nose and shook his head. "Fine, but let's make this quick. I don't wanna be working all night."

"Trust me; the feeling is mutual."

We drove down Route 299 and stopped at the last bar before hitting the Thruway exit. It was empty and quiet inside. A middle-aged man greeted us at the door as we flashed our badges.

"How can I help you?" the man asked.

"We're hoping you or a member of your staff could help us. We're looking for two girls that may have been at your club the other night. We were wondering if someone here might remember seeing them."

"I'm the only one here right now. But you're more than welcome to come back later tonight and talk to my staff."

Lombardo nudged me and pointed to the cameras. "What about those?" he asked. "You think we can get a look at them to see if we can find our missing students?"

"Sure, if you think it could help."

"We do. Thank you," I replied.

We followed the manager to the back and where he looked up the tape for the night in question. "Please, let me know if there's anything I can do to help your investigation."

"Don't worry; we will," Lombardo snapped before walking briskly out the door.

"That was rude," I called out between breaths as I tried to keep up with his long strides to the car.

"Look, we got what we came for, and this guy wasn't able to tell us shit. I figure we better get our asses back to the station and go over all these tapes."

We both knew it was going to be a long night. Even if we watched the tapes from ten until the bars closed it would estimate four to five hours of footage to comb through per tape. There was six bars/clubs to investigate which meant we were stuck for the next ten to fifteen hours watching drunken college kids acting stupid, dancing, and doing their best to get laid.

I popped in the first tape while Lombardo took one from the pile and reviewed it in another room. I fast forwarded the recording to ten that night and hit play. Within an hour I saw something that caught my eye. Our victims entered the club.

I paused the video and ran to the next room, pounding on the door until Lombardo let me in. "I found the girls on one of the tapes."

"Which one?"

I smirked as I told him it was the last bar we visited. He opened his mouth to say something but knew he was screwed no matter what was said. Instead, he closed his mouth and followed me back to my room.

We played the video and did our best to find the girls throughout the night on the video. There were too many people packed inside and we couldn't see the girls unless they went up to the bar.

"There they are," I said excitedly as I pointed to them leaving the bar forty minutes later.

"And they're alone," Lombardo replied. "Now, we're back to square one. This was a waste of time."

"Not necessarily. It was still early in the night. Maybe they went to another bar."

"Great, another wild goose chase. Let me know when you *think* you found something again."

It was another few hours before either of us spoke to each other. I was on my second tape after seeing the girls walk away from the first club. Meanwhile, Lombardo had just finished reviewing his first video. He nearly scared the crap out of me when I heard him yelling twenty minutes into the recording.

"What? What happened?"

"I found them." He pumped his fist in the air in triumph before hitting play on the remote.

We watched in silence as our two victims were standing with two men near a pool table. We couldn't hear anything that was said, but kept staring at the four of them. One of the two men had their hands all over Sandy. The other man looked apprehensive about making a move on Brenda.

We watched the four play pool for a few minutes before seeing the larger of the two men drop something into three out of the four drinks before handing them off to the unknowing recipients.

"Tha-that's gotta be them," I said in a stunned whisper.

We watched the video a little longer and saw the larger man carry out his date followed by his friend and Brenda. They stumbled through the doors and down the block, but we couldn't see where they went.

"Those are our guys." Lombardo seemed angry and I didn't understand why. "We need to find those assholes and bring them in."

"Agreed, but we need to bring Ricky in on this one."

"Fuck him; this is our case."

"It's partly his. The captain wanted us to work with him."

"Fine; make the call."

I dialed Ricky's number, but he was out and was told they didn't know when he would be back. I knew Lombardo was going to love hearing that bit of news. To cover our asses, I called the captain and let him know what we found. We were told to do nothing until he got there.

The captain arrived a half hour later with Rodney at his side. "Okay, Ryan, you better have something good to share."

We played him the video and told him those two girls were the latest victims, and the two men in the video are suspected to be the last people to see them before the girls went missing.

"What's your plan of action?" the captain asked.

"I think we should stake out Main Street and wait for these guys to show up. Maybe check in with the bars before they get busy to see if they recognize the suspects or could let us know if they see them."

"Sounds like a decent plan, but I have one better. If these men are still in the area, they may look for their next targets relatively soon. We need to be ready to grab them the first time they show their faces at another bar."

"What are you suggesting?" Lombardo asked.

"I'm sending officers to each bar in New Paltz tonight and will coordinate with the surrounding towns to do the same. We'll do this every night until these assholes show their face. Johnson, I want you to coordinate a team for the New Paltz locations."

"What about us?" Lombardo snapped. He seemed to think the same thing I did; that the captain was ripping the case away from us.

"You two will be going out tonight and will lead the team."

That was a bit of relief, but I swore my bar hopping days were behind me. I really didn't expect to go through them again with Lombardo by my side.

Knowing I was in for a long night, I decided to go home to get ready for a night on the town. I put on a tight little black dress and a pair of heels to make it look like I was going out to party. On the outside, Ali Ryan was ready to have fun and get trashed, but under the dress, I had my cuffs and gun strapped to the inside of my leg with my badge tucked inside my clutch.

I decided to let my sister know I wouldn't be home until late that night. When I opened her door, I found half the room had been packed up and ready to be moved to some unknown destination. I was sad to see she was leaving me, but knew she needed to be on her own, even if I thought it was a big mistake.

I headed for the door, but found a tired and worn out looking man that resembled my boyfriend. Although, we hadn't talked much since he came home late and drunk the other night.

"Hey," he said while looking me over. "Where are you going?"

"Out," I replied.

"Out where?"

"I have a stakeout tonight."

"Looking like that?"

"Yes. What's wrong with what I'm wearing?"

"You trying to pick up some dude at a bar?"

"Maybe, if I'm lucky." I smiled to let him know I was joking.

"I'm glad you find this funny, because I definitely don't. Ali, where are you going?"

"Not that it's any of your business, but we got a lead on the kidnapping case and are going to a few bars to see if we can locate our suspects."

"You're going with Lombardo?"

"Me, Lombardo, Rodney, and about half of the Ulster County police force. Do you have any more problems?"

"Yeah, I wanna go too."

"Sorry, you're not working this case, but I'm sure your ex would love to keep you company tonight while I'm out."

"Ali, for the last time; there's nothing going on between us."

"And it better stay that way if you know what's good for you."

"Babe, you're the only one I wanna be with."

"Then I suggest you hurry up and finish your case so you can kick the bitch to the curb and we can enjoy our vacation."

"A week with you on a beach in a bikini during the day and spending all night with your sexy ass is all the motivation I need. I'll have this shit done in a week."

"I'll hold you to it." I started walking out the door. "So, I'm guessing no meeting or undercover work tonight?"

"Nope, I was planning on spending the whole night with you, but I guess I'll have to wait until you get home."

"Maybe I'll wake you in a special way."

James wrapped an arm around me and pulled me close. He pressed his lips against mine firmly and let his tongue sweep over mine. "You better get back here soon. I want more of this later."

Damn, can I call in sick? I definitely don't wanna go out to the bars after getting kissed like that.

Chapter 22-HT

Javier sat in the passenger seat of the white van waiting for Dimitri to get back from his meeting with their drug dealer. He needed to grab his roofie of choice before hitting the bars for the night.

The time alone gave Javier the opportunity to think of how he planned on making good on his promise to Valentina. He needed to find a way to get her out. She was running out of time. The schedule the previous girls had been on took weeks to get them hooked on the drugs, trained to be sex slaves, and played with by nearly every guy on the boss' payroll before they were interviewed and prepped for the bidding. Valentina had been there for just over a week and had already been fast-tracked to the prepping.

Javier wanted to appeal to the boss' human side in hopes he might show some compassion. Instead, he was forced to watch Valentina be humiliated as she was stripped down in front of strangers, photographed and videotaped as she divulged her sexual history. Worst of all, he witnessed Dimitri taking advantage of Valentina while she was in a vulnerable state only to antagonize Javier for some sick pleasure.

"Yo, loverboy," Dimitri shouted as he snapped his fingers in front of Javier's face. "Wake the fuck up. You need to be on your game tonight."

"Relax, I know what we gotta do."

The boss had called him earlier while Javier sat in the security room staring at Valentina through the monitor. He was told to go out and pick up two more girls, stating he needed an ebony goddess and a self-entitled rich girl to complete his collection for the auction. But Javier knew better; they were to satisfy the boss' cravings.

"So which do you wanna go after tonight?" Javier asked.

"After getting your bitch nice and wet, I need someone I can break until they're begging for my cock."

Dimitri's comment further fueled the fire burning inside Javier. He'd love nothing more than to do the world a favor by putting a bullet in Dimitri's head.

"Dude, just shut the fuck up and drive."

"Come on; I'm just busting your balls. You need to lighten up."

"I really don't need advice from you right now."

"I'm just sayin; you're letting some chick fuck with your head. It's like she's got your balls in her purse and you're not even dating her."

"Are you done? I'd like to find a bar so we can get to work. I don't feel like spending the whole night in New Paltz again."

"Fine, but don't pick some random chick just to end the night. Have fun and enjoy yourself."

They turned off of Main Street and parked the van on a side block. They walked back to one of their favorite bars, knowing it would be packed with women. They split up to cover more ground, with Javier hoping Dimitri would score early enough to call it a night , but he had a feeling it wouldn't be his lucky night.

Javier surveyed the crowd while circling the dance floor from the safety of the walls. He didn't want to make a move until he found what he was looking for, but there were no ebony goddesses at the bar that night. A few girls caught his attention. Had he not been so smitten with Valentina, he might have acted on pursuing them for a fun night at a motel room.

Standing around wasn't helping Javier. He was miserable while he watched others having fun. He realized a big part of him wanted to be part of that too. He finally broke down, grabbed a drink from the bar, and searched for one of the blondes that caught his eye.

He started dancing near her and slowly made his way closer until he was eye-to-eye with the girl. She didn't seem to mind as she took a step towards him. He did the same and leaned forward to put his arm around the girl's waist.

"What's your name?" the girl asked.

"Javi," he replied. "What about you?"

"Danielle."

Javier smiled and pulled Danielle closer until they were grinding each other on the dance floor. He could feel his body respond to her touch. It was like she brought him back from the land of the dead with her body.

"You wanna get a drink?" she asked.

"Sure; let's go."

They pushed their way through the crowd until they reached the bar. He had an eerie feeling someone was watching his every move, but chalked it up to Dimitri spying on him.

The bartender placed their beers and shots on the counter and took the money. Javier knew he needed to bring a girl back, but fought the urge to lace the beer with the drugs Dimitri picked up earlier in the night. He decided to see what happened with Danielle and hoped he could have one night where his life felt normal.

As they walked back to the dance floor, Javier felt the presence of someone following him again. He knew someone was watching him, but couldn't see past the countless dancing bodies. His eyes darted around the room, finding a tall, curly-haired brunette with her eyes locked on him.

He doubted whoever it was knew him or what he did for a living. He had been careful every time not to linger long enough for the victims' friends to get a good look at him and typically tried to avoid surveillance cameras whenever they went to a bar. He continued dancing with Danielle, but kept watch for the woman spying on him. He saw her getting closer and caught a glimpse of her face from one of the rogue neon colored spotlights.

Fuck, he thought when he recognized the woman was none other than Detective Ali Ryan. He knew her from all the articles about her infamous takedowns of three serial killers. If she was at that bar, he was in trouble.

"Hey, I'll be right back. I gotta take a leak." Javier disappeared into the crowd and frantically searched for Dimitri. He was hitting on the girl from the frat party with hair as dark as coal. He studied her face and saw a similarity between her and the cop he was running trying to run away from before she caught up.. He slapped his hand on Dimitri's shoulder. "Dude, we need to get out of here now." There was panic and urgency in his voice as he spoke.

"Don't tell me you struck out already."

"I'm not playing, man. This is an emergency."

"What the fuck are you talking about?"

Javier glanced at the girl who had her eyes closed and could barely stand. "We have a code blue on our hands. We need to run."

The duo had set up code blue to mean the cops were in the building. If one of them mentioned it, both were to find the nearest exit and run like hell.

"You sure?" Dimitri asked.

"I saw her myself. It's that famous one that's been all over the news and in the papers."

"Shit!" Dimitri looked around nervously. "I already slipped this bitch the drug. What the fuck do we do?"

"Leave her. The boss would rather we get back empty handed then get pinched for trying to bring home some bitch from the bar."

Dimitri didn't say anything to the girl. He left her standing in the middle of the dance floor by herself, but Javier stood by her side and tried helping her to a table.

"What the fuck are you doing?"

"If we left her standing there, she'd drop to the floor and cause a scene. You really want to deal with that on top of the cop being here?"

"Yeah, cause then at least the bitch would be focused on helping the drugged up whore than searching for us."

"Fine, I'll do it myself and meet you outside."

The girl wrapped her arms around Javier's neck and held on as he moved her towards an empty chair. "Hey there, hot stuff. I'm Amanda. What's your name?"

Javier closed his eyes. Hearing the name confirmed his fear. The woman chasing him through the bar was Detective Ryan, and the girl hanging on to his neck was her sister.

"Just call me trouble, cause that's what you'll be in if you run into either of us again, especially my friend." He pulled Amanda's arms free and placed her into the chair before scurrying through the crowd. He met Dimitri down the block. They walked quickly back to the van, checking over their shoulders as they rounded the corner.

"You're sure it was her?" Dimitri asked as they darted onto Route 299. "I mean I was getting ready to take that hot piece of ass home for a couple of rounds before letting the boss have his fun. I'd hate to have left such a fine looking girl behind for nothing."

"Trust me; it was her. I've seen her in the papers. I know what she looks like. It can't be a coincidence she was there tonight."

"You think she knows who we are?"

"Maybe, but I'm not taking any more chances, especially since that girl you drugged tonight was her sister."

"Shit, and you pulled me away from her?"

"I guarantee if you touched her sister, you'd have a bullet in your head by morning."

"We took the lieutenant's daughter and they haven't found us yet. You really think she'd figure out where we took her sister?"

"With this cop, I wouldn't put it past her. She took down three serial killers and killed two of them because they fucked with her and her family. Word on the street is she didn't kill number three because he was already in handcuffs."

"You know people blow shit out of proportion. I doubt she did all that herself."

"I don't wanna take that chance. So, we either need to change where we hunt for girls, or get the fuck outta town."

Chapter 23-Ali

I met Lombardo and half of the Ulster County police force a few blocks from Main Street. We kept our distance so we didn't freak out any college students or scare away our suspects. The captain left us in charge of covering New Paltz, but tasked Rodney to enlist the help of the Dutchess County P.D. to cover the bars across the river.

Everyone was dressed to party. Some of the officers wore jeans and t-shirts; others wore khakis and a polo. The females wore jeans and tank-tops, or they wore skirts. I was the only one wearing a dress. All eyes nearly bulged out of their heads when they saw me get out of my car.

"Damn, Ryan," one officer called out. "Who knew you had that hiding under your dress pants and button downs."

A few others cat-called me while I approached. "Don't make me have to kick your ass in a dress. I really don't want your blood staining it," I replied. "Now enough of the bullshit; let's get to why we're here tonight."

"Each of you have been assigned a bar," Lombardo interrupted. "You are to go inside and blend in with the crowd."

"Does this mean we get to drink?" an idiot shouted from the back of the group.

"Oh you can buy a drink, but you better make sure it's non-alcoholic." I could hear the groans as I laid down the law. "Sorry guys; we need everyone sober tonight."

"Ryan is right. We need everyone on their game tonight. If these guys are still in the area, we don't want them catching wind that we're onto them. You've each been given a picture of the suspects. If you see them, radio into us so we can help you take them down. There's no telling what these men are capable of and it's unknown if they're armed."

We broke up into our teams. Unfortunately, the captain thought it was best to keep Lombardo with me and gave us Officer Dina Moreno to be part of our team. We entered the bar separately. We didn't need anyone to know we were there together. We needed to keep the men out of the way while the women were to pose as bait.

I walked around the bar for a half hour dancing and sipping on my virgin daiquiri. No one seemed to stand out as someone trying to drug any girls. I kept searching the crowd for anyone resembling our suspects, but it was impossible to see a face from ten feet away let alone from across the room.

I kept moving to the beat of the song when I was approached by guy in jeans and an open button down shirt. He grabbed my hips and dragged me towards him while he tried to grind on me.

"No thanks; I'm not interested," I said, but I couldn't tell if he was ignoring me or just couldn't hear what I said. I leaned in and said it again loudly in his ear. His arms tightened around me as he lunged to kiss my neck. I shoved him back. "What the fuck part of no don't you understand?" I turned to walk away and felt his hand grab my ass. I spun around quickly, kneed him in the balls and knocked him out with one punch. "Maybe next time you'll learn to listen." I stormed away from the guy before attracting a crowd.

I approached the bar and found Lombardo standing there ordering a drink. "I thought we're supposed to stay sober tonight?" I asked.

"Ali, you really think these guys are gonna show up here right after they abducted two girls? We're here wasting our time. I might as well have a beer or two to get me through the night."

"I really don't know if they would come out tonight, but four out of the five girls we know they kidnapped were taken from bars and parties in this area. So, yeah it might be a waste of our time, but I'd rather be safe than to let another girl be abducted by these assholes."

I walked away without ordering my next round. I didn't want to be there watching everyone else have a good time. I could've been home with James making up for the last week of not seeing each other. But we had a job to do and I was dead set on finding our suspects even if I had to stay there all night.

I fought my way back through the crowd only to be hit in the shoulder from some jackass who was in a hurry to get to the bar with some chick he must have just met.

"Asshole," I shouted but the guy ignored me. I stared at him for a moment and thought he looked familiar. I took out my phone and searched through the pictures we had of our suspects. Sure enough, he was the apprehensive guy playing pool the night before Brenda and Sandy were taken.

I followed him and tried to get close enough to see if I was right. By the time I cleared the crowd; they already ordered their drinks and paid. The man seemed to stare at his companion's bottle which made me even more suspicious. I was certain it was one of the suspects. I opened the group text and typed I may have one in my sights. I followed them through the crowd until they stopped to dance. I felt my phone buzz. I looked down and saw a text from Rodney.

R: Did James say he was going out tonight?
Me: No, he told me was staying home. Why?
R: He's at the bar I'm at dancing with some chick.
Me: Does this chick have red and black hair?
R: Yeah, I think so.
Me: I'm gonna kill him when I get home. Get me a picture of them.

I was enraged. *The son of a bitch told me he was staying home and would wait for me to get back. That liar.* I didn't care what his excuse was; there was no reason he should've been out at a bar or club with Jocelyn at midnight. I had so much anger and hatred fueling through my body that I didn't notice the suspect had fled and left the girl he was with standing by herself.

"Where did the guy you were with go?" I asked.

She seemed a bit lost and confused. "What? Who are you?"

I reached into my cleavage and pulled out my badge. "I'm a cop, and the man you were just dancing with is a suspect in a kidnapping spree. Now, where'd he go?"

"He said he was going to the bathroom."

I fought my way through the crowd and found Lombardo pacing by the bar. "Where is he?"

"I lost him. The girl he was with said he was headed towards the bathroom. Go check it out and I'll stay by the door."

Lombardo ran to the back and started pushing people out of the way as he entered the bathroom. He returned a minute later red in the face and anger in his eyes. "Fucker must've seen you and split."

We raced outside and saw the bouncer standing by the door. "Hey you see either of these guys hurry out of here?" I asked while showing the picture of our suspects.

"Yeah, they left a couple of minutes ago."

"Where'd they go?"

"Around the corner; haven't seen them since."

"Thanks," we replied in unison as we tried to follow their path. It was a steep road to travel. I took my heels off and rushed down the pavement barefooted with Lombardo chasing after me.

"You see them?" Lomabrdo's voice boomed in the night sky.

"They're gone."

"Fuck," he screamed as he kicked someone's tire. "You had him in your sights. What the fuck happened?"

"I glanced at the phone for a minute and he was gone."

"One shot…this was our one shot to grab one of them and you blew it because of a damn phone."

"Yeah, because I was trying to call for backup." It was a lie and I knew it. I blew the investigation because of Rodney telling me about James and Jocelyn dancing at a club together.

Lombardo threw his hands in the air. "I'm done."

"What do you mean?"

"I mean I'm going home. If the guy you saw was one of our suspects, then he and his partner are already on the road and there's no telling where they went."

"We can't give up on finding them."

"Ali, the damn thruway is a mile down the road. They could've gone in either direction or taken Route 299. There's no way we can track where they went without knowing what they're driving."

"They're probably driving the white van they used to pick up Valentina from JFK."

"You mean the one with no plates? Yeah let's put out an A.P.B. on a white van with an unknown plate number." Even I could tell how stupid my plan was, but hearing Lombardo say it made me feel like an idiot for even thinking it. "Besides, we don't know for sure that's what they're driving."

"So what do you propose we do?"

"I'm going home. You can do whatever you want." Lombardo walked back to his Jeep and took off without saying another word.

The remaining officers gathered around looking for guidance, but I had nothing to say. "You heard him; go home."

I hung around the bar scouting the area for any sign of our suspects. It was doubtful they would return. Hell, if they thought we were there they'd be complete idiots to ever come near New Paltz again.

I stood at the corner for about ten minutes before walking back to the green awning. I wanted to ask the bouncer a few more questions, but was sidetracked by my sister being dragged out of the bar by one of her girlfriends.

"What the hell happened to her?" I asked.

By the look in her friend's eyes, she knew I was Amanda's way overprotective sister. "I-I think she had one too many," the girl stammered.

My sister knew her limits and hadn't been this trashed since she mourned the loss of her previous boyfriend after he was hit by a train meant to kill her.

"How many did she have?"

"I-I don't know."

"What do you mean; you don't know?"

"We were having a few drinks and she ran into a guy she recognized from a party the other night. He offered to buy her a drink and that was the last I saw of her until a few minutes ago."

Shit, my sister was in the same bar as the kidnappers. She could've been their next target…maybe she was their next target.

"Where's her boyfriend?"

"I don't know. He said something about having to work late tonight and told her to go out with the girls."

I wanted to take Amanda home, but I knew she would wake up and pick a fight with me for dragging her back to my place. I couldn't ask

Rodney to take care of her because he was still staking out the bars in Poughkeepsie with the Dutchess County P.D.

"Give me her bag." I took the clutch from Amanda's friend and quickly grabbed her pink cell phone. I scrolled through the contacts until I found Lucas's name. "Hey, it's Ali. I need you to do me a favor and meet me in New Paltz. Amanda is really drunk and I'm working a case out here."

"Yeah, sure. I can be there in a half hour."

I did my best to keep Amanda awake which proved to be incredibly difficult. The way she drifted off, I wondered if she was that drunk or if someone slipped something into one of her drinks.

A half hour later, Lucas pulled up to the bar. He helped me place Amanda into the passenger seat and reclined it to let her sleep.

"What the hell happened to her?" he asked.

"I don't know, but she'll be safer with you tonight."

"No offense, but I'm not the one carrying a gun."

"Yeah, but I have some things to take care of tonight and can't be worried about her. At least she'll be in good hands with you."

"Thanks, Ali."

"You can thank me by keeping an eye on her. A lot of shit has been going down at the bars and clubs around the area and I don't need to worry about her getting caught up in it."

"You know I can't keep her from going out."

"Then you better make sure you're with her when she does."

I kissed my sister's forehead and watched Lucas drive away. I stuck around a little longer and followed up with the bouncer and the bartenders. No one seemed to notice anything strange, which meant I was getting nowhere with my investigation.

Having no choice but to admit defeat for the night, I decided to go home. There were no cars parked in the driveway, and the lights were off inside. Seeing the emptiness only confirmed what Rodney texted me earlier. I hadn't checked my phone since I saw the suspect had fled. I checked it before opening my car door and saw another message from Rodney. It was a picture of James standing at the bar with his arm around Jocelyn's waist. She was wearing a short skimpy dress and leaned in, no doubt she was trying to kiss him.

I wanted to start the car back up and race to that bar, but I knew Rodney wouldn't tell me where to find them. He knew I would cause a scene or end up in jail for beating the hell out of her. Another part of me wanted to drive and just never look back. If Valentina and the lieutenant weren't counting on me to find her, I might've taken that trip. Instead, I entered the house and turned on the lights.

A single rose lay on the bed. There wasn't a note or any sign of James in the house. He may have been trying to plan something, but was tempted by whatever offer Jocelyn made him. That thought was the final straw. I was done with being the nice one. I was done taking crap from everyone, and I was done with James.

I took his pillows and threw them out of the bedroom. Then I started on his closet, ripping his clothes out and leaving them in a pile in the living room. By my third trip out there, he entered the house with his face full of shock.

"Ali, what the hell?"

"You tell me, James. Where the fuck were you tonight?"

"I was out."

"Out where?"

"I went out to a club for my investigation."

"I thought you didn't have anything planned for tonight. I thought this was supposed to be a night off from it."

"Yeah well, things change. I got a call about an hour after you left from the guy we're investigating. He wanted to meet for some drinks. So I went out there, had a couple of beers, danced a little and came home."

"Who were you with tonight?"

"I just told you."

"Who were you really with, James?" He looked at me and stared. The way I was grilling him, he must've figured out I knew the truth. "Tell me; did the guy you were investigating call or Jocelyn?"

"Ali, you're getting the wrong idea. There is nothing going on between us."

"Was she there?"

"Yes, but-"

"But nothing, James. You lied to me. You told me you were staying home tonight and I find out you went out with Jocelyn instead."

"It was for the investigation."

"Yeah, it's always for the investigation. If that were really the case, then why didn't you call or text me to let me know you were going out?"

"Because I knew you were on a stakeout."

"Then why not leave a note here?"

He shook his head and took a few steps towards me. "Ali, I'm sorry. I didn't expect to get that call tonight. I rushed to get ready and ran out the door. I should've texted or left a note."

"You were just too much in a hurry to meet up with your ex; right?"

"It's not like that at all. You need to calm down and let me explain."

He tried to grab my hand, but I yanked it away. "Don't touch me." I backpedaled to the bedroom and slammed the door before he could try to stop me. He tried to enter the room, but it was locked.

"Ali, come on; open up."

"No, James. I'm done dealing with this shit right now. Good night!"

"Wait, where the hell am I supposed to sleep?"

"The couch if you're smart, but I'm sure Jocelyn would love to welcome you back to her bed."

"For the last time; there's nothing going on between us."

"You keep telling yourself that; maybe you'll believe it one day."

Chapter 24-HT

Javier woke up the next morning remembering the previous night's events. He allowed himself to go after something he wanted, even if it was in the form of another barfly. But the girl he met wasn't the typical college student who went bar hopping to look for some guy to buy them drinks or someone that was searching for a hookup. She was closer to her mid-twenties and dressed more conservatively than most of the women in the bar. Although he wanted to get to know the girl more, he was derailed by the presence of Ulster County's infamous detective.

Seeing Detective Ryan at the bar was like throwing him into a pool of ice water. It forced him to put the brakes on his night out. He had felt like someone was following him for a few minutes, but when he saw the look in her eyes, he realized she knew who he was.

He barely told the girl he met some lame excuse about running to the bathroom, but he needed to get Dimitri out of there before the detective found him with her sister. He already laced her drink with the drug and would've dragged the girl outside had Javier not intervened.

He did everything to persuade his partner to follow him immediately, but for a second he considered leaving him there to take the fall. He was sure Dimitri would've ratted Javier out instantly and told the boss to move everyone before the police showed up. But there was no way he was willing to take the chance of letting another girl fall victim to their game. He forced Dimitri to leave and narrowly escaped the police without fulfilling the boss' agenda.

Seeing Detective Ryan at the bar stirred up something in Javier. He knew she was getting closer to finding out his name, but didn't think she could pinpoint his location. He also knew Valentina was running out of time and would be sold to some rich asshole. No one would ever see her again, and he needed to do something about it.

He considered acting on those thoughts that morning, but received a call from the boss that sidetracked him.

"I need to see you in my office, immediately." The tone in his voice was filled with disappointment. He must've realized how Javier failed to acquire the two last pieces to the shipment.

Javier got dressed and made his way to the office. The boss welcomed him inside while he sat behind the desk.

"You wanted to see me, boss?"

"Come in and have a seat."

"Look if this is about last night-"

The boss waved him off. "It was an unfortunate situation, but not one I feel we need to worry about. I believe the police were there looking for men that were abducting women. I have no reason to believe they were looking for you and Dimitri specifically."

Javier wanted to tell the boss how wrong he was with that statement. Detective Ryan had him in her sights. He was just lucky enough to escape.

"I know. I'm just sorry we couldn't deliver the last two girls you requested." It was a lie. Javier was happy he didn't have a hand at ruining two more innocent lives for the boss's financial gain.

"I wouldn't call last night a complete loss. Your buddy Dimitri went back out last night and picked up the ebony goddess I requested."

Shit. I can't believe he went back out after they nearly got busted. He was more pissed he dragged another woman back to the complex than risking the rest of their safety and freedom. "That's great news. Then, we just need one more girl."

"No, it's not necessary. This acquisition is more than enough to fulfill the shipment. I will personally see to the new girl's training for the next couple of days."

"Is there anything you need me to do today?"

"Yes. I need you to prep the auction room and alert the stylist. Our young pretty guests will be put on display this afternoon."

"Why so fast? Don't you want some time to train the newbie?"

"She will be fine. Besides, I want to cash in on the lieutenant's daughter before the cops get too close. Do you have a problem with that, Javier?"

"No, sir. I'll get everything ready."

Javier exited the room and alerted their stylist they needed to get the girls ready for the auction. He ordered a small team of men to set up the room for that afternoon, but he made a slight detour before joining them.

Javier entered the building where the women were kept and told the man watching the security cameras to take a fifteen minute break. Once the guard was gone, he slipped inside the room and found Valentina in a pool of sweat.

"Are you okay?" he asked.

"I'm not feeling too good."

Javier slipped a small syringe from his pocket with a lower dose he had been giving her and injected it into Valentina's arm. "I need you to listen to me. My boss is moving forward with his plans and is going to sell you and the rest of the girls here to the highest bidder."

Tears streamed down Valentina's face. "You promised you would get me out of here."

"I will; I have a plan, but you need to do exactly as I say."

"Why should I trust you?"

"You have every right not to, but I don't wanna see you get hurt. I've seen too many girls come through here and sold off to men and taken somewhere no one will ever see them again. I'm sick of destroying lives and I'm ready to answer for the things I've done."

Valentina laid there letting Javier's words sink in. "What do you need me to do?"

"I've been lowering your dose of the drugs so you have more control, but I need you to go through with everything I tell you today as if you were still completely drugged out of your mind."

"Why?"

"I need to buy some time to put my plan in action, but the boss won't let me out of here until after the auction. So, I need you to act like you are still under our control."

"And what's supposed to happen at this auction?"

"You and the rest of the girls are going to be dressed up, have your makeup and hair done. Then they'll bring you ladies in one-by-one into a room. There will be video cameras covering every inch of the room. You will model and do whatever they ask of you, including taking your clothes off."

"I have to get undressed in front of these pervs?"

"Unfortunately, yes you will. They will want to make sure they aren't buying what they call damaged goods. Some are picky about tattoos and scarring, they want to make sure the girl on display is exactly what they want before the bidding begins."

"How long will this take?"

"It's usually about a half hour per girl."

"And where will you be?"

"I'll be on the opposite side of the door escorting the girls back here."

"So then what's this plan of yours to get me out of here?"

"I plan on meeting with someone tonight. I think given the circumstances, she will be more than happy to help me if it means saving you."

Chapter 25-Ali

I woke up alone in the bed, just like I had for most of the last week and a half, but this time it was by my choice. The fight with James last night was bad. Maybe I was overreacting, but I think catching your boyfriend out with another woman, especially an ex, when he was supposed to be home is grounds to be pissed off.

I didn't want to get out of bed. My world seemed to be caving in around me. I was stuck on a case with a guy I hated, my boyfriend may or may not have cheated on me with his ex, and the lieutenant's daughter was still missing and I let the only suspect we had on the case go because I was preoccupied with texting Rodney.

It was still early, but I wanted to leave without waking James. I hurried to get dressed and tiptoed through the house. I found him lying on the couch with his leg draped over the arm and the other over the headrest. I snapped a quick picture in case I decided to forgive him and have something to torture him with later.

I was almost out the door. My hand was turning the knob when I heard him say my name in a sexy raspy voice. "Ali, where are you going?"

"I need to get to work."

He looked at his cell. "But it's only seven."

"I need to go in early since I blew our only lead last night."

"What? How did that happen?"

I pulled up the picture Rodney sent me on my phone showing James with his arm around Jocelyn. "I was a little preoccupied."

"Shit. Ali, I'm sorry; it's not what you think."

"Save it. I'm sick of hearing you say that every time I catch you and her together. I can't do it anymore."

"What are you saying? Are you breaking up with me?"

"I don't know, James. But whatever is going on affected my investigation last night and I can't let that happen."

"So, that's it; you're calling it quits on us."

"No. I'm just not dealing with whatever this is right now."

I made a haste exit and ran for my car. I wanted James to come running after me; to fight for me; to fight for us. He knew where I was headed and could easily show up right as I pulled into the parking lot. But I needed him to stay away. I needed the time to pull myself together and put an end to the human trafficking ring. The only way to do that was without him being around to distract me.

I arrived at the station by seven-thirty and found several officers getting ready for their shift. I didn't want to be bothered by them or anyone, including the lieutenant. I approached my desk to grab the case files, but they were missing. "Did anyone touch the stack of folders on my desk," I called out.

"Yeah," someone replied. "Lombardo was sniffing around your desk and took them into one of the conference rooms."

"Thanks."

I briskly walked down the hall until I found Lombardo half asleep reading over the files. "What the hell are you doing here?" he asked when I entered the room.

"I could ask you the same thing."

"I'm working."

"Yeah...well...that's what I'm here to do too."

"Great, sit down and go over this pile again." He shoved a stack of folders towards an empty chair. I could tell he was still pissed at me for what happened last night.

"Look, I'm sorry about-"

"I don't give a shit what happened. We lost our only suspect and now we need to figure a way to track him down. Now, do you wanna help or did you wanna waste time talking about things we can't change?"

"Okay, let's get to it."

I read through the first three files within ten minutes. It was the same information we looked through about fifteen times. It was pointless. There wasn't anything in them that we didn't already know.

"What's the matter?" Lombardo finally asked.

"Do you really think sitting on our asses going over the same files we've been looking at for almost two weeks is going to help us?"

"What do you want me to do, Ali? Our only lead was right there in the same building with us and we let him slip away."

"I know; I'm sorry."

"Save the apology; I don't want it. What we need is for you to get your head out of your ass and be the hot shot detective everyone says you are."

"Since when do you think I'm a great detective?"

"I don't, but everyone else seems to think you are. So here's your chance to prove me wrong."

I sat there digesting Lombardo's words. He was challenging me to do the impossible and find suspects that seemingly were off the grid. That's when it hit me.

"Can you do a search for abandoned warehouses, apartment complexes, and offices?"

"Sure, but why?"

"The other night, Rodney and I were following up on a lead Ricky gave me." I saw the anger in Lombardo's eyes as I admitted I withheld information from him. "We spoke to a security guard who said he saw a random car showing up at this small abandoned warehouse every night. Every time he went to check them out, they drove off in a hurry. The night before we met him, he said there were several cars there including a limo. What if they used it to sell the missing girls?"

"But why check out abandoned buildings?"

We can't seem to find anything about our suspects; not a name or an address. What if they're hiding out with the girls in a place where there is no owner?"

"Okay, but what about foreclosed houses?"

"People going in and out of an abandoned house would look suspicious, and parking a big white van on the property would really get the neighbors talking."

"So you think they took over some abandoned facility?"

"It makes sense. They would need someplace big enough for the girls they kidnapped and themselves, it would have to be a place inconspicuous enough to hide their van, and be far enough away that if a girl escaped, they couldn't run to the next door neighbor to call the cops."

"Say your theory is correct; it'll take forever to go through each facility until we find the right one; if we find it at all."

"I know, but that's a starting place. You wanted me to prove you wrong; well then, this is how we do it." I got up to leave the room.

"Wait, where do you think you're going?"

"I'm paying the bar another visit. Maybe I can get the footage from last night and we can review it to see how the suspects escaped."

I ran out of the station hoping Lombardo would have everything pulled up by the time I returned. I called the owner of the bar while I was on the road and asked them to meet me. I told him about our suspects showing up last night and needed the footage to track them down. He was more than willing to help considering the circumstances.

"You sure they were here last night?" he asked as he popped out the tape from the night before and handed it to me."

"I saw one of them with my own eyes. He slipped through the crowd when I tried to call for backup and got away."

"Then take this and put that son of a bitch behind bars. We need this town to feel safe again."

"That's exactly what I intend to do."

I returned to the station an hour and a half later and signaled for Lombardo to follow me. We queued up the tape and watched the progression of the night as we waited for the suspects to appear.

They first showed up on camera around the ten-forty-five mark. They were two men; one was a tall muscular man with short dark hair. The other was average size with jet black hair. He wore glasses, but I didn't remember seeing him with them on when I saw him dancing with the girl.

The video continued to play for the next three and a half hours as we watched every angle the cameras gave us, hoping for a better view of our suspects. The best shot we had was when they bolted from the bar. It was the best picture we had of our suspects.

"We need this picture sent to be analyzed. I want to know who they are and where we can find them."

Lombardo looked at me as if I was a three headed dog named Cerberus. "Excuse me," he said loudly.

"Sorry," I replied. "But you wanted this side of me."

"Then your ass better deliver." He got up from the table and walked out of the room. He returned a few minutes later with a folder and slapped it down next to me. "Here are the listings. I think you might wanna give your security friend a call and have him help you narrow this shit down a bit."

"Thanks, I'll give him a call from the road. I was about to grab a late lunch/early dinner. You want me to bring you back something?"

"No, I'm good."

"Then, I'll be back in an hour."

I rushed out the door. I didn't want to leave, but I skipped breakfast and had been sitting at the station doing work for too many hours without having any food in me.

I tried calling the number Ricky provided for Victor, but the call kept going straight to voicemail. It was odd, but chalked it up to him falling asleep without charging his phone. After my third failed attempt, I drove to New Paltz and stopped to eat at the Gilded Otter. I was starving, and decided it was best to eat lunch and grab something for later. I loved their quesadillas and decided to order it while asking them to make the southwestern grilled chicken breast to go.

I sat in silence waiting for my food. It was the first time in almost a year since I could say that about my life. Everything was usually thrown into chaos. I heard a buzzing and looked down at my phone. Rodney's name was flashing. *So much for silence.*

"How is my favorite partner doing today?"

"Ali, I've got some bad news."

I didn't like the tone in Rodney's voice. I knew when he was messing around and when he was serious, this was one of those times where I needed to shut up and listen.

"Okay, lay it on me."

"Last night one of the cops I partnered with got a call for a homicide in Wappingers Falls. It was late, so I decided to tag along to see if I could help. When we got to the address, I found a security car with no driver in it."

"Rodney…"

He took a deep breath and sighed. "We found Victor beaten and bloodied on the opposite side of the warehouse he was stationed at last night. His tongue was cut out and left for us to find." Rodney took another deep breath. "He was dead before the ambulance showed up."

"You think our suspects did this to him?"

"If he was found outside his car or if it was shot up, I'd consider alternatives. But this was personal. Whoever did this brought him to the spot he described to us, the one with all the cars. And no one cuts out a tongue unless they wanted to send a message."

"I'm assuming Dutchess P.D. is all over that case."

"I told them what I knew hoping they would let us work with them, but I was told to go back to my station."

"Thanks, Rodney. I'll bring it up to the captain when I get back." Before I could say another word, my cell was ripped from my hand. The thief pulled out the chair across from me and sat at my table.

"Um, excuse me," I snapped. "Can I help you?"

"No, but I'm here to help you."

I glanced up at the stranger. His face had been etched in my mind since last night, and now he was sitting across the table from me.

"You!" I reached for my gun, but the man sat back and held his hands up in the air.

"I'm not here to harm you; so let's not doing anything foolish."

"Why are you here? And how did you find me?"

"I followed you from your station. I needed to get you alone, and if I walked in there I was going to end up in jail."

"How do you know that's not where you'll end up in a few minutes?"

"Because you wanna hear what I have to say."

I knew it was the man from the bar. It took everything in me not to beat the hell out of him in front of everyone and arrest him. But he was offering to talk, and I was curious to hear what he had to say.

"You better make it good, and start with your name…your real name. I don't want some alias or some fake bullshit."

"My name is Javier Contreras. And based on your expression, you know I'm the one who kidnapped your lieutenant's daughter."

I clenched my fist, fighting the urge to swing at him. "Okay, Javier; what do you want?"

"I want to make things right."

Are you fucking serious? "And how do you plan on doing that?"

"By asking for your help. I wanna help Valentina and the rest of the girls escape, and I want my boss' operation to be shut down for good."

"Why should I believe you want to help us?"

"Because I'm here, ready to tell you everything I know instead of helping them sell the girls and get out of town like the boss wants to do."

Javier confirmed Valentina was still safe, but told me they were about to move the girls very soon. Whatever he wanted to do, we needed to act fast.

"Why do you wanna help us?"

"It's because of Valentina. Following her sparked something in me; a desire to want more from life than having more money than I know what to do with. Grabbing her from the airport made me think I could have a life with her, but I know that can never happen."

"So you fell in love with her?"

"Yes, but she also made me see what I've done was wrong. We have destroyed so many lives. I can't live that life anymore."

"Did you have this revelation before or after you killed Victor Sims?"

"Who?"

"Don't play dumb with me; you know exactly who I'm talking about." There was a blank expression on Javier's face. "He was the security guard that stumbled on your rendezvous with some rich assholes driving fancy cars."

"Detective, I don't know who you're talking about, and I sure as hell didn't kill anyone."

"Someone working for your boss did last night. They left him to die in the same spot he saw your deal go down."

"If it was someone from our organization, I didn't hear about it."

A part of me wasn't sure if he was telling the truth, but something in his eyes seemed genuine.

"Fine, you said you wanted to help. What exactly do you want in return for your assistance?"

"I want to help you bring his organization down. You get the girls we took and the ones that are still around as servants to my boss. I'll serve him, his friends and associates on a silver platter. I can get you all the financials and anything else you need to put them behind bars for the rest of their lives."

"I also want the name of the person that killed Victor."

"I'll see what I can find out."

"And in exchange you want what?"

"I want my freedom. I want to know what it's like to truly live a life that doesn't involve kidnapping and selling women."

"So you want immunity?"

"I just want a second chance to live my life."

"I can't promise you anything, but I'll see what I can do."

"Good, that'll give me some time to get what you'll need to take down my boss."

"You still haven't told me his name."

"You get the deal in place, and you'll get his name and his head on a silver platter along with all his cronies."

"And I'm supposed to let you go based on your word."

"You should trust me. Your sister was almost a victim last night."

"What the fuck is that supposed to mean?" I slammed my hands on the table and stood up. "Are you threatening my sister?"

"No, but if it wasn't for me, she would've woken up this morning next to Valentina."

"You better keep talking or you're not leaving here in one piece."

"There were two of us at the bar last night. Dimitri was off trying to find his own action last night. When I saw you, I grabbed him to leave. He had already drugged the girl he was talking to. I saw the resemblance and figured she was your sister. I forced him to leave and made sure your sister was safe at a table before I left."

I grabbed Javier by the throat. "You knew she was drugged and you left her by herself. You realize how vulnerable you assholes made her; what could've happened to her?"

"The alternative was much worse, I assure you." I release my hold and moved back to my chair. Javier reached into his pocket and pulled out a vial. "This is what we used to drug the women into coming back to the complex with us. You can use this as collateral for my word."

"You realize I can easily just follow you back to the hole you crawled out of and take everyone down in one shot without your help."

"You could, but then I wouldn't be able to guarantee the girls would be safe or that you would fry the real players in this game."

I slowly reached for my bag and pulled out my card. "You have twenty-four hours to call me with some sort of plan or evidence to give me and my team."

"He held the auction earlier, which means the boss plans on moving the shipment in two days. I'll get the details and let you get your team ready."

Javier got up from the table as my quesadilla arrived and slipped passed the waitress. He timed everything just right to ensure I couldn't follow him. Whoever he was, Javier was smooth and had things planned perfectly, which made me wonder if he had slipped up at the bars on purpose so he would get caught. Was it all designed to bring us to the face-to-face meeting? If it was, he had me looking forward to hearing his plan to take down his boss.

Chapter 26-Ali

I had the waitress pack up my food and bring everything to me in one bag. I doubted I would eat at all after having a bombshell dropped on me. I didn't waste any time. I hurried back to my car and rushed back to the station. I called Lombardo from the road while speeding down Route 299.

"You won't believe what just happened."

"Ali, I don't have time for your games."

"This isn't a game. I stopped for food and our suspect from last night followed me to the restaurant."

"Tell me you got him."

"Not quite. He sat down at my table and wanted to talk."

"Talk about what?"

"He wants to help us take down the organization and save the girls."

"And let me guess; you bought it?"

"I didn't buy anything. He promised to deliver the five missing girls, and would hand over enough evidence to guarantee a conviction against his boss and all his friends. He also gave me a vial and said it contained the drugs they used on the girls to get them to come back with them."

"For all we know it could be water in that vial."

"Then have an analyst come down to the precinct and I'll have them test it. He also inadvertently confirmed they were hiding in a complex."

"Fine, let's say he's telling the truth; are we letting this guy off the hook for his involvement? I mean; I'm sure he's asking for immunity."

"He is, but I told him we couldn't guarantee anything."

"Good, we need to-"

"We need to bring Ricky and the captain in on this to consult."

"Are you nuts? Why do you want to include them? This is our case."

"Ricky let us in on the Port Authority's investigation. I want the captain in on this too. I want to make sure this goes down the right way so no one gets off on a technicality." I could hear him let out a loud breath of air. "You wanted me to do whatever it took to end this investigation; this is how it gets done."

"Fine, what do you want me to do?"

"Get the analyst there as soon as you can. I'll be there in five minutes. I'll call the captain and Ricky when I get there."

I pressed harder on the gas as I past the New York State Thruway exit and barreled down Route 299. I pulled into the parking lot and rushed into the station. I breezed past Rodney and went straight into a conference room. I pulled out my cell phone to call the captain but saw a text message from an unknown number.

J: I just got word the deal is going down tomorrow night in Poughkeepsie. I won't get the address until late in the afternoon.
Me: Send me the info as soon as you get it.

I called the captain and told him about my encounter with Javier and what he wanted from us.

"You do everything to ensure this deal happens. I don't wanna lose him, the girls or a chance to stop these men from abducting any more women."

"So you want us to broker the deal?"

"I'll make a couple of calls. I don't care if we let one scumbag go to take down his boss and buyers. I'll call you when you can go down, but you better have enough to get the warrants and get the deal signed."

Lombardo walked in as the captain hung up on me. He had his arms folded over his chest. "What's the verdict?"

"Captain said to make the deal."

"Are you serious?"

"He wants us to do everything we can to take down this human trafficking ring and save the girls."

"What about your buddy?"

"I haven't called him yet, but I'm sure he'll want to be part of the takedown as well. Do we have an ETA on the analyst?"

"He should be here in a twenty minutes."

"Good. We need them to put a rush on it."

There wasn't much I could do except wait. We couldn't move until I got the call from Javier. I needed the captain to give me a call back to tell us who we needed to talk to regarding the immunity deal and the warrant to make the necessary arrests.

Inside of a half hour, the analyst arrived and took the vial to be tested. He told us it would be at least a day before they would have the results. I understood, but wished we could have everything we needed before facing a judge or the D.A.

We waited for two hours before the captain called back. "Ryan, get down to the Poughkeepsie police station right now. I set up a meeting between you, the D.A. and Judge Heyman."

"I'll be there in an hour."

"Make it thirty minutes. I know your driving reputation."

"Fine, but I don't wanna hear Lombardo bitch about it."

"Just deal with it and I'll talk to him later."

I hung up and smiled at my partner. "Looks like I'm driving."

We jumped in a cruiser and sped down Route 9W until we crossed the Mid-Hudson Bridge. The red and blue lights swirled in the early night sky. The siren forced drivers out of our way as I drove into Poughkeepsie.

"Now I know why Rodney hates driving with you," Lombardo smirked as we exited the car.

"You can thank me later."

"Oh I'm sure I can take you."

I got in Lombardo's face. "You couldn't handle me."

"There's only one way to find out."

"Name the time and the place."

"We end this investigation and you're mine."

I laughed in his face and walked inside the precinct. It had been a while since I stepped foot inside the Poughkeepsie station. I forgot it was the same station James worked out of, and prayed we wouldn't run into him. But there was no way I would get lucky twice in the same day.

We rounded the corner to meet with the D.A. and saw James talking with Jocelyn. "Ali," he said as he looked up.

I shook my head, trying to tell him it wasn't a good time, but he kept walking towards us. "I don't have time for this," I finally said.

"Ali, wait; we need to talk."

"No, we don't. I'm here on business."

"It's okay, baby," Jocelyn said loud enough for me to hear her. "You don't need her when you have me."

I lost my composure. I had endured enough of their bullshit and couldn't keep my mouth shut any longer. "You keep coming after James, yet he's always back home with me every night."

"That's only after I've had my way with him."

"Trust me; he wouldn't touch your skank ass after the things he told me about you." He told me a few things but kept most of it to himself, but she didn't need to know.

"We'll see who he prefers once our case is over." She looked up at James and slowly led him away. "You'll love what I'll be wearing tonight."

I tried to go after them. I wanted nothing more than to kick her ass and didn't care if she decided to press charges for it. I wanted to make sure she knew not to touch my man. I took two steps and felt a hand close around my wrist, dragging me inside an office.

"You wanna beat the hell out of her? Do it on your own time. We're here to get the warrants and deal you requested. Don't let some bitch get under your skin and derail you."

"You think I'm gonna let her go near my boyfriend-"

"For now, you have no choice. Too many people are depending on you. The captain wants this deal, so you need to make it happen."

I knew he was right, but that didn't stop me from wanting to beat Jocelyn into a bloody pulp "Fine, but if I see her once this is done, you won't be able to stop me."

"We get the bad guys, and you can kick her ass from now till next year and I won't say shit to stop you. Hell, I might make some popcorn and enjoy the fight."

"You're a pig."

"Oink-oink, baby. Now let's get this over with; I want this done."

We found the D.A. lingering around Lieutenant Guinn's office. We sat down with him and hammered out a deal that was contingent on the information Javier provided, the safety and return of all five missing girls, and the arrest of the unnamed boss and all his associates. We needed him to fulfill all three conditions of the deal in order to get his immunity.

It took us longer than we expected, about two hours longer to be exact. By the time we finished, the judge had already left. We had the deal ready to be signed, but no warrant to execute our arrests.

The next day we returned to visit Judge Heyman. He graciously agreed to meet with us before court was in session to ask for his assistance.

"Your Honor, we have a source within a known human trafficking ring willing to help us rescue several abducted women as well as turnover evidence that will put his boss away for life."

"Great, where is the evidence?"

"We haven't received it yet."

"Then what do you have?"

I approached the bench and presented him with a folder filled with the information surrounding the missing girls, how and where they were taken, and the deal in place for Javier.

"This is everything?" Judge Heyman asked.

"Yes, sir. We should have more this afternoon, but our source said they are moving the women tonight."

He skimmed through the information and stopped on the file for Valentina. "Is this Lieutenant Esposito's daughter?"

"Yes, Your Honor. She was abducted from the airport about two weeks ago. She is one of the five we will be rescuing."

Judge Heyman closed his eyes and took a deep breath. "Against my better judgment, I'll grant your warrant, but you better not make me regret this decision."

"We won't, sir."

"Good. Now if you'll excuse me, I need to make a call to your lieutenant to check on him."

I wanted to ask if they knew each other, but I think his decision already answered my question. He was granting us the warrants we needed as a favor to the lieutenant so he could be reunited with his daughter.

When we exited the building, I saw James walking up to the building with Jocelyn trailing behind him. The moment we locked eyes, the little bitch quickened her pace and grabbed James to make it look like they were holding hands.

"Ali, don't," Lombardo said as I marched down the path to meet them halfway.

James must've realized what happened and shook himself free. "Ali, she just grabbed my hand. I swear; nothing's going on."

"That's not what you were saying last night," Jocelyn interrupted.

"You're right; he was shouting my name while we fucked in our bedroom." I said it a little too loud, but I wanted her to know she was nothing to him, even if I did need to tell a little white lie.

"You know; he won't stay with you for long. He'll find his way back into my bed. He always does."

I balled up my hand and was ready to knock her out on the front lawn of the court house. I felt Lombardo sneak up behind me ready to pull me back the moment I lunged at her.

I shook out my hand and relaxed. "You keep telling yourself that, sweetheart. The only way he'd ever go back to you was if I was dead and buried. Even then, you'd be nothing more than a consolation prize, but I'm sure that's not the first time someone looked at you that way."

Jocelyn lunged at me, but was quickly restrained by James. I'm sure he knew what would've happened to his asset if she hit me, and that could've cost his investigation.

"Enough, Joss. You need to go inside and wait for me. I'll be there in a few minutes. I need to talk to Ali." We waited for her to walk away and towards the police station. Lombardo excused himself as well. "I'm sorry about her. Trust me; I can't wait for this case to be over. Maybe then, we can get back to normal."

"James, we never had normal. Chaos is our version of normal."

"Yeah, but that's not what I want for us."

"What do you want from us?"

"We can start with you and me lying on a beach somewhere. After a week of having you all to myself, then we can come back here and start planning for our future."

"I like the sound of that. How much longer do you have on this case before we can make the dream a reality?"

"We're almost done, babe; I promise. Another day or two and we should have this investigation in the bag."

"Good, because I want you all to myself."

James leaned in and planted a sweet romantic kiss on my lips. "I liked what you said about fucking me till I screamed your name. Maybe we can work on that tonight."

"It'll have to wait until I get done with work. We just got the green light with our investigation."

"You mean; you're taking them down tonight?"

"Yeah."

James looked excited and worried. "Maybe I can get special clearance to join your team. This way you have someone watching your back that you trust." He looked over my shoulder at Lombardo.

"Weirdly enough; I actually trust him now. Besides, Rodney and my friend Ricky from the Port Authority will be there as well."

"You know I won't be able to sleep until you get home?"

"Damn, and here I was hoping to wake you in a special way."

"You're killing me, Ali."

"And you love every minute of it."

"God, help me; I do." He gave me another quick kiss before telling me he had to go inside. I allowed him to run off. But I was now one hundred percent focused on our case and more determined than ever to end this once and for all.

Chapter 27-HT

Javier knew sitting down with Ali Ryan was a bad idea, but he also knew it was his best chance to set the girls free and get out of the shitty life he made for himself. He hoped it was the right decision, and that he could stop the boss from hurting any more women.

He had promised Detective Ryan everything he could in order to guarantee himself immunity. He fully planned on delivering every bit of what he said. He didn't offer it for his freedom; it was to save his life. If the boss managed to get free, make bail or if he beat the charges, Javier knew he was a dead man.

He rushed back to the complex and tried keeping to himself. He waited until the others were occupied by their jobs before he made his way to the small building where he frequently met the boss.

It was dark when he entered the office, knowing full well the boss was tending to personal business. Javier entered quietly, keeping the lights off as he used the spare key to infiltrate the inner office. It was once a place he enjoyed visiting, but now it was stained with the memory of Dimitri violating Valentina with his hand and by recording her while she stripped off her clothes. It strengthened his resolve that he was making the right choice.

He rummaged through the drawers and made copies of the files he and the boss made regarding the women they had locked up. He logged onto the computer and made duplicates of the financial transactions and the videos of the girls they currently had, as well as the women they had previously sold. Everything had been backed up on an external hard drive, and now it was ready to be handed over to the police.

Javier made a quick exit and hid the hard drive inside his jeans to ensure no one saw what he was concealing. He hurried across the parking lot to his apartment and deposited the device under his mattress. Javier had everything he needed, except one thing.

He made one more trip to across the lot and entered the building where the women were kept. He checked the security station and found the guard sleeping in the chair. It was typical for the night crew to doze off as nothing good ever happened at night. He crept across the hall and slipped inside the room, finding Valentina instantly.

He covered her mouth and tried to keep her calm as she tried to scream. "It's okay; it's only me."

"What the hell do you want?"

"I met with your father's friend today."

"What friend?"

"That detective he's obsessed with; Ali Ryan."

"How did you meet with her and are not sitting in prison?"

"I made a deal. I'm getting you out of here…all of the girls actually."

"How?"

"I have a plan, but I need you to trust me. Shit's going down tomorrow, so you need to be ready."

"You really talked to Ali?"

"Yeah, and for a minute I thought she was going to blow my head off when she reached into her bag."

"Yup, that's Ali."

"Well, I hope that's not how she treats everyone who tries to do her a favor."

"You deserve it after the hell you put me and these other girls through."

"You're right. I know I'm a douchebag, but I also care about you."

Valentina scoffed at Javier's remark. "You're just trying to cover your ass so you don't go to jail."

"If that were true, I would've taken you up on your offer for a blowjob when you were desperate for a fix, but I didn't want you that way. If I were to ever be with you, I'd want you to choose to be with me, and not just because you were going through withdrawal."

"I don't know what to believe."

"You don't have to believe me; I just need you to trust me tomorrow. Then, if you want me gone, I'll leave and never come back." He bent down and kissed her forehead before walking back to the door. He crept back to the security booth and found the guard still asleep.

He slowly backed away, bumping into another man who reeked of sex. He looked up at the man and jumped back. "Boss, what are you doing here?"

"I should be asking you the same thing."

"I-I was just checking up on everything before going back to my place for the night."

The boss clapped Javier on the shoulder. "Good man, but you need your rest for tomorrow night."

"Don't worry, sir; I'll be ready to go."

"Well, just to make sure everything goes off without a hitch, I think I may join you."

This was the first time the boss was present for an exchange. "Are you sure? I mean; you never attend."

"Yes…well, I want to make sure our little virgin is handled with extra care. I wouldn't want something to happen to her, now would we?"

"No, sir," Javier replied. He was worried the boss no longer trusted him and that could cause a problem at the exchange.

The boss wiped the sweat off his face. "That last girl Dimitri brought me is a little hellcat. I kind of wish I hadn't sold her so quickly. I would've liked to go a few more rounds with her."

"I know the feeling," Javier lied.

They walked out of the building together, but the boss veered off towards his office. Paranoid thoughts consumed him as he wondered if the boss would notice if something was slightly out of place, or if he had remembered to turn the computer off. He feared going to bed. If the boss found something out of place, his suspicions would grow and he knew he would be labeled a suspect.

He entered the apartment but kept watch by the front door, waiting for the boss to leave. The lights turned out in the office shortly after as he left for the night. Javier started to relax when he heard a knock on the door.

"What do you want?" he asked while staring at his unwelcomed guest. It was taking everything in him not to slam the door in Dimitri's face.

"I thought I might come by and see if you wanted a smoke or some beer." He held up the six-pack in his hands and offered a cigar.

"I'm really not in the mood."

"Then take five minutes and listen."

"I don't wanna hear what you have to say."

"Yeah, you do, because last week, I was in your shoes."

Javier focused his attention on Dimitri and snatched one of the cigars from his hand. "Start talking; you have until I finish this."

"You were right...about me and Eve. I got too emotionally invested in her and didn't want to let her go."

"What's this got to do with me?"

"You're doing the same with Valentina."

"Can you blame me? She's such a hot piece of ass."

"Don't do that...don't belittle her or your feelings for her. I know what you think and what you want every time you see her."

"You don't know what you're talking about," Javier said while blowing out a puff of smoke.

"I have a better understanding than you think. I was ready to die for Eve the night she was delivered to that rich piece of shit. I wanted nothing more than to put a bullet in his head the moment he touched her."

"Why didn't you?"

"Because I knew you would stop me. I also knew the boss would find out and kill me on the spot."

"Why are you telling me all of this?"

"Because I know Valentina is special to you, and I wanna help."

"Help how?"

"I got the name and address of the guy that took Eve. We can make the drop with the current batch of girls and make a run for it with Valentina. We can track down Eve and steal her back too. Then, the four of us could find a place to live our lives together."

"There's one big problem with that plan."

"What's that?"

"The boss said he's coming to the exchange tomorrow night."

"What the fuck? He never-"

"I know. He fed me some bullshit about wanting to make sure she's kept safe and the exchange goes through properly."

"He thinks you'd run off with her?"

"Yeah, I think so.

"Then we need to come up with a plan B."

"I already have one.'

The next day was spent getting ready for the shipment. The girls were sent to the stylist to have their hair and makeup done before being handed their dresses. Javier paced the property waiting for the boss to tell him where the exchange would take place. He hadn't heard from him all day. In fact, no one had seen or heard from the boss since the night before.

It worried Javier when the van pulled up to take them to the drop without speaking to the boss first. It wasn't right, it wasn't normal. Dimitri stepped out of the driver's seat.

"You ready to go?" he asked.

Javier didn't know what to do. "We're still waiting on the boss. No one's heard from him all day."

"He called me a half hour ago and said something came up. He told me to go in his place." He leaned in and whispered to Javier. "I guess we can do what we talked about last night."

"Yeah," he reluctantly replied. "Did he tell you where to bring the girls tonight?"

"Yeah, we're meeting in the back of a hotel right before the I-84 exits. It's perfect for our escape."

"I don't know; something about this seems all wrong. I think you need to hang back here."

"No way. They'll kill you if shit gets fucked up and you're alone. I told you last night I have your back and I plan on sticking by my word."

Javier looked down at his phone as Dimitri entered the building to get the women. He brought up the text messages he sent Detective Ryan and contemplated his options of who he would side with and who he could trust.

Chapter 28-Ali

I spent most of the day waiting for a call or a text to come in, telling us when and where the exchange would be made. It was getting late. We were all restless. No one knew where we had to go, or how fast we would need to get there. For all I knew, we would receive the location and would arrive too late.

"I told you he was full of shit," Lombardo said with a smirk.

"You don't know that for sure."

"Ali, he led you on."

"Then why did he give me his name?"

"It was probably some fake name to get you to lower your guard so you would trust him. He probably set this whole thing up so we would spend the day sitting on our ass instead of hunting him down. I bet they already made the exchange and are already out of the state."

I walked back to my desk and grabbed a file off my desk. "Yeah, take a look at this." I slapped the folder against Lombardo's chest.

He opened the file and skimmed through the pages. "Is this legit?"

"Yeah, it is; so much for him giving me a fake name."

"So, he was stupid enough to give you his real name. It doesn't mean he's going to come through tonight."

"You wanna put money on it?"

"Don't do it," Rodney advised. "I've lost more money to this woman than I care to admit."

"She's not getting her hands on my wallet."

"What's the matter, Lombardo; you scared?" I asked.

"I'm not afraid of anything."

"Then put your money where your mouth is."

"Fine, name your price."

"Hundred bucks?"

He was just about to shake on the deal, but something caught his eye. I turned around and saw the phone on my desk glowing. I checked it and saw a text message from the same number that contacted me earlier to say their boss was coming to the exchange as well.

"Is it him?" Lombardo said with skepticism.

"Actually, yeah it's our guy. He just sent me the address of the meeting and said we have an hour to get there."

"Where is it?" Rodney asked.

"It's a hotel off of Route 9 in Fishkill. I-84 is right around the corner from it. If we're even a second late, we could lose them."

"We need to move," Lombardo commanded. He was right, but I knew we technically had to wait. "What the hell are you doing? We need to go."

I dialed a number on my phone. "Lieutenant Guinn, this is Detective Ali Ryan."

"I wasn't expecting to hear from you. What did Detective Dumbass do this time?"

"Nothing, sir. I'm calling because I need a favor."

"I'm not really in the business of doing favors, Detective."

"Well, tonight's a perfect time to start. I'm working on a huge case and we just found out our suspects are meeting in Dutchess County."

"And let me guess; you want me to sign off on you conducting your investigation in my jurisdiction? Tell me; what's in it for me?"

"For starters, you'd be helping to put away kidnappers and rapists behind bars. Also, my lieutenant's daughter is among the women about to be sold. So, you can either help us out and get his daughter back, or we can let him know you're the reason his daughter was sold into being someone's sex slave."

"Are you fucking serious? I'll send some of my guys to help; just send me the location."

I didn't trust Guinn to help us. I was sure he wanted to send his men in to get the glory of the bust and to be the one to save Lieutenant Esposito's daughter. But there was no other choice; we needed someone to ensure no one left the meeting.

I told him where to send his officers and pushed Lombardo out the door. I told him we needed to make sure we weren't stepping on their toes.

"You wasted time over that shit?"

"I was covering our asses," I replied as we piled into a car. Rodney and Lombardo weren't fond of me driving, but there wasn't any dispute on who would get us there the fastest.

We rushed to get into Fishkill, pulling into the lot twenty minutes before our time limit. I found the Dutchess County P.D. exiting their unmarked cars.

"Has anyone shown up yet?" I asked.

"No," they replied. "Are you sure your source said it was this hotel?"

I grabbed my cell to look over the text again, but saw a white van drive past us. It was the same one from the video the day Valentina was taken from the airport.

"That's gotta be them," I said while pointing to the passing vehicle. We jumped in our cars and followed the van, leaving enough room behind to make sure we weren't noticed. We watched them pull off the road. When we drove by, I saw they entered a restricted area blocked off by a metal blockade with stop signs attached.

We waited another fifteen minutes before another car showed up. I could see Lombardo was getting impatient. His leg bounced up and down while fidgeting in his seat.

"We need to go in," he snapped.

"No, we can't until the rest of them show."

"And what if this guy leaves with one of the girls before the others show up?"

"Then we have one of the cars tail them."

"Fuck this; I'm going in."

"Wait," I shouted. "Look, we've got company."

Another two cars drove down Merit Blvd and turned where the white van had earlier. There were three sitting ducks that unknowingly walked into our trap. I sent a text to the number asking how many more they were waiting on to show. He told me there was only one more expected buyer.

Lombardo sat back in the passenger seat and tried to wait a little longer. After another fifteen minutes, he became increasingly annoyed and started snapping at Rodney and me every time we spoke. At the rate he was going, I didn't know if he would survive another ten minutes before I knocked him out. Thankfully, we didn't have to put that to the test as another pair of headlights pierced the darkness and pulled into the same spot as the other guests. The text came in instantly from Javier telling us everyone was there.

"Okay, lights off and move in quietly," I called across the radio. We moved the cars slowly in front of the exit and kept out of view. We turned off the engines and swept the front of the lot, finding empty cars and a building ahead.

I signaled to the others and fanned out to make sure there were no guards watching the grounds while their transactions took place inside. We crept under the half boarded up windows while circling the building until we had all exits covered and were sure there weren't any surprises waiting for us.

Me: Breaching the building

I held up three fingers and counted them down slowly. In one fluid motion, a dozen officers busted into the small building with our guns ready to fire on anyone who even looked like they were about to attack us.

"Down," some of the officers shouted.

"I wanna see hands in the air," a Dutchess cop shouted.

The buyers and their drivers complied instantly. The women dropped to the floor, covering their heads with their hands. The only men still standing were Javier and a tall muscular man standing next to him. I saw him reaching for his waist and shook my head at him, trying to tell him to stop. He grabbed the butt of his gun and ripped it from his pants. He had a shot lined up. He was about to pull the trigger and put an end to Lombardo. I tackled my partner to the ground just as Javier did the same to the gunman.

"What the hell are you doing?" the large man said.

"Don't do it; they'll kill you."

"The boss will do the same if we get pinched."

"You need to trust me'" Javier wrenched the gun from the man's hand and pushed it along the floor towards us. He stood up with his hands in the air. A handful of officers rushed both men, slapping a pair of handcuffs on each of them.

Once I realized we were safe, I jumped off of Lombardo and rushed to Valentina's side. She was wearing a white lacy dress with a long slit up the side.

"You're okay now," I whispered. "Are you hurt?"

"No, Javier did his best to take care of me. Are you arresting him?"

"Yes, for now."

"Bu-but he said he made a deal with you."

I pulled her aside and brought our voices down to a lower volume. "I did, but he still needs to make it look like we're taking him in for now. Don't worry; we're going to take care of him."

"What about the others?"

"What do you mean?"

"That creep they worked for and the rest of his goons?"

There were more of them? I moved towards Javier and dragged him off the ground. "I thought your boss was supposed to be here tonight."

"He was; he never showed, but I have everything you need to arrest him back in my apartment."

"You're staying here for now until we get everyone back to the station. Then, we can worry about grabbing the information from your apartment."

"No, it'll be too late. He'll know something's up if we're not back in the next hour. If he catches on to what happened, he'll run and take all the money with him."

"So, I'm supposed to just let you go?"

"Follow me if you want, but if we don't move fast, you won't get another chance to take him down."

"Fine, but I'm going with you in the van." I whispered to Rodney what the plan was and told him to send another team to the address Javier just gave me. I wasn't going to let the slime ball slip through my fingers, especially after what he put Valentina through for the last two weeks.

Chapter 29-HT

Javier was forced to watch Dimitri get carted off with a pair of cops. They shoved him into the back of a patrol car, which sped off down the road.

"Your friend is gone," Detective Ryan said. "It's time you make good on the rest of your word. I want the son of a bitch responsible for the hell these girls went through."

"Fine, let's go," he replied.

They jumped in the white van and pulled onto the road. He sped back to the complex hoping to get there before anyone caught wind of everyone getting busted. People were bound to find out. Five of the boss' big name buyers were arrested while trying to buy kidnapped women as sex slaves. Once their names were released to the public, the media would be all over their cases.

"You know she asked about you," Detective Ryan said.

"Who did?" Javier replied.

"Valentina…she wanted to make sure we had a deal in place and that you would be okay."

Javier couldn't help but smile. There was hope in his eyes. *Maybe I didn't fuck this up like I thought.* "Well…am I going to be fine?"

"As of right now, you made good on your promise. If you deliver the other half, you've got your freedom waiting for you back at my precinct."

"Thank you."

"You're the one putting your neck on the line to save those women. We owe you a great deal of gratitude."

"Then why did I feel like your team wanted to kill me?"

"Can you blame them? You helped abduct the lieutenant's daughter and kidnapped countless other women over the span of god knows how many years."

"I've been working for my boss for the last five or six years. I lost count as to how many women my partner and I grabbed for him. But once I get the files, it should help tell you where most of them are or should be."

"What do you mean?"

"These men buy the girls to use as their personal escorts and fuck toys. When they get bored, they pimp them out to their friends or sell them off to another colleague or associate. I can't guarantee if anyone over six months ago will still be with their original buyers. They might not even be alive."

"And somehow you feel like you can justify what you did to them?"

"I guess I used to, but not anymore. Back then, I just cared about the money and having sex with beautiful women that were around to take orders from me. But after meeting Valentina, I wanna do whatever it takes to make things right."

They turned down a steep path and traveled down a pitch black road. The first sign of light was from the side of the complex.

"This is where you kept the girls?"

"This is where we all live," Javier replied. "You should probably get in the back where no one will see you."

The detective complied with his suggestion as he turned into the complex. He drove to the back lot and parked as if he was about to unload a new shipment of women.

"Wait here until I get back," he ordered. "I should only be about five or ten minutes."

Javier exited the van and stopped as he took one more look at the office. He could see the light was on inside and decided he was about to take down the man who tried to sell his happiness. He glanced back at the van and pointed ahead to the office building.

He stormed down the path, ready to break down the door. He needed to calm down and lure the boss into a false sense of security. He entered the office and smiled as he saw the boss about to turn off his desk lamp.

"Javi, you're early. I didn't expect to see you for another ten or fifteen minutes from now."

"We got done early and wanted to make sure you were okay."

"I'm fine," the boss replied. "Why do you ask?"

"I thought you planned on being a part of the exchange tonight. When Dimitri showed up in your place I got a little worried something might have happened to you."

"As you can see, I'm just fine. I had an unexpected business meeting to tend to and couldn't make it to the exchange." He put a caring hand on Javier's shoulders. "How are you holding up?"

Javier almost forgot he was supposed to be upset. Valentina was supposed to be with her buyer, but he made sure that never happened. He had forgotten to appear sad or angry. Instead, he was trying to make conversation as if nothing bothered him.

He lowered his eyes and brushed the boss's hand away. "I'm not gonna lie, I'm pissed, but I understand. This is business, not a place to find a wife."

"Exactly," the boss replied. "Now if you'll excuse me, I have a few things to take care of before going home."

"Maybe I can help you. I found something, or rather someone, I think you might enjoy. I have her knocked out in the back of the van."

"You picked up a girl tonight? After making the exchange?"

"Yes, sir. I thought you might like her."

The boss was curious and walked around his desk. "I'll be right there; I just need to do one more thing. He opened a drawer and pulled an item from it. "Oh, before you go, I have one more request."

"What's that?" Javier asked.

"Die!" The boss pulled the trigger, firing the bullet directly into Javier's head. He was down with one shot. The boss bent over him and looked at the lifeless body as a pool of blood formed around Javier's head. "I know what you did yesterday. I know who you spoke to and how you betrayed us tonight. Sucks you'll never get to be with your love now."

Chapter 30-Ali

I heard the gunshot. It's easy to become accustomed to the sound when you're a cop, especially if you hang out at a gun range. But I've heard it too many times over the last few months.

Without hesitation, I slid open the side door and started off in the same direction Javier took. I was only a few feet from the van when I saw someone walking around on patrol. He took one look at me and shouted, "Intruder."

He whipped out a pistol and mere seconds before he could aim I had my glock pointed at him and fired. The guard was down before he could even think about pulling the trigger, but that just drew more attention to me.

Half a dozen men swarmed around their fallen comrade with guns clutched tightly in their hands. I knew I could take out one, maybe two without getting hit if I was lucky. The moment their eyes flickered towards me, I no longer had the upper hand.

I raced around the van, hoping to use it as a shield as the men began firing their weapons. I jumped through the open door and crawled to the front seat, praying Javier left the keys inside, but there was no such luck. I quickly dialed Rodney from my cell.

"Rodney, what's the ETA on my backup?"

"Ali, what's going on?"

"I'm taking fire. I need my backup now."

"There's already a team about ten to fifteen minutes out."

"I don't know if I have fifteen minutes."

I placed the phone down on the floor of the van and crept towards the back. I glanced around and saw one of the men reloading. I took aim and fired, hitting him square in the chest. I ducked back before his buddies saw me.

"One down; I have five more," I said loud enough for Rodney to hear on the phone.

"Ali, you need to get somewhere and hide until backup arrives."

I crept back towards the front of the van and opened fire again, wounding another in the shoulder.

"Rodney…Rodney are you still there?"

There was no answer. I was left for dead while waiting for backup to arrive. I could hear the barrage of bullets colliding with the side of the van. There wasn't anything left of the windows but shards of glass. I was screwed. There were five men still armed and targeting me. All I had to defend myself was my gun and about ten bullets.

The gunfire stopped momentarily and I could hear the men whispering to each other. I wondered if they were low on ammo and were trying to figure a way to trap me. I looked down and realized my feet were probably visible to them. If I was right, there was nowhere for me to run without them seeing which direction I was headed. I had no other choice. I needed to make a run towards the buildings for cover or else I was a sitting duck.

I took a few steps back and bent down to see if I could use the same trick to see where they were hiding. I hurried to my right and fired a few shots, wounding another goon. I could hear them coming and zigzagged as fast as I could towards the buildings behind me. I was nearly there when I tripped over the curb and landed hard on my side.

I could see the group of men slowly walking towards me. Their numbers seemed to have grown despite the one I killed and the other two I wounded.

I could see a couple conversing while two of the men had their weapons pointed at me. I raised my gun, but they shook their heads.

"I wouldn't do that, sweetheart. You're way outnumbered."

I was prepared to die as long as I took half of these assholes with me to hell. I closed my eyes, said a little prayer under my breath, and was thankful the gunshot I heard was accompanied by the blaring siren of a squad car.

The goons turned their head at my backup as bullets flew through the air. I opened my eyes quickly and pulled the trigger, putting an end to the asshole standing over me. With the last few rounds, I helped the officers take down the rest of the goons effortlessly. Once they were down, I laid on the ground staring up at the sky, thanking god for answering my prayer by sending help.

I heard more sirens pull into the lot as a man knelt down beside me. He cupped my head in his hands. "Ali...baby, tell me you're okay."

I recognized the voice and opened my eyes to see James. "What are you doing here? How did you find me?"

"Rodney called. He said you were in trouble and backup wasn't there yet." His hands patted my body. "Are you okay? Were you hit?"

"No. I fell over the stupid curb and twisted my ankle."

"You're kidding; the great Ali Ryan was almost killed because she tripped over a curb."

"Shut the hell up." I playfully smacked him and planted a kiss on his lips. "So, how did you get here so fast?"

"Did you forget how fast I drive?"

I was well aware of his need for speed. He showed me several times with the top down on his car. It's what made me open up to James in the first place, and I was damn happy he put it to good use that night.

"Are you two all right?" a booming voice said as a giant of a man stood over us.

"We're fine, Rodney," I replied. "But we need to find out what happened to Javier."

"They found him inside one of the smaller buildings. Someone put a bullet in his head. I guess his boss figured out what happened."

I sat up and shook my head. "So, we'll never figure out who his boss was or where Javier hid the information he was about to turn over."

"Hey, you might crack one of the goons we arrested," James suggested. It wasn't a bad idea, but didn't know if I could continue pursuing the investigation. It was the second time in a few weeks I narrowly escaped death. I didn't want to push my luck for a third time.

Epilogue

A week had gone by since the shooting at the complex. It was a week of hell for me as I had been interviewed several times by Internal Affairs, the captain, my lieutenant, James' lieutenant, and had to give my deposition for everything I encountered over the previous two weeks. They also benched me for a few weeks due to the shooting, and because I shouldn't have been on active duty following the capture of Officer Reyes. There have been a lot of things I shouldn't have done, but I always did what I wanted. This time, I allowed them to bench me.

The lieutenant gave me two weeks paid leave. It was perfect timing because James just finished his case and no longer had to work with his ex-girlfriend anymore. We had two weeks of being together, and planned on making the most of it.

The other night, James came home and let me know our flight and hotel were booked. We were two days away from escaping New York and heading to the Bahamas. I was ecstatic and couldn't wait to go on a real vacation.

I packed a few things, mostly bathing suits, a few pairs of shoes, and a couple of dresses. Based on the way James talked, I didn't think he would let me wear any of it. I wasn't surprised and loved the idea of being his for entire two weeks.

The day before the flight, James left a voicemail telling me he had a surprise for me when he got home from work. I spent the day with my sister, but decided to get back a little early. I didn't care what James had in store for me, but I planned on surprising him with some sexy new lingerie.

I didn't see any cars in the driveway when I got home. I entered the house and saw red rose pedals lining the path from the door down the hall to the bedroom. There was a bottle of champagne sitting in a bucket of ice on the counter in the kitchen with two empty flutes. I popped it open and filled the glasses. I took a sip from one as I walked down the hall.

"James," I called out.

I decided to follow the path to the bedroom. I opened the door with a smile on my face as the bed was filled with more rose pedals.

"I'm glad you like it, Detective," a voice said from across the room.

I turned to my left and saw a man sitting at the desk in my bedroom. I grabbed my gun and pointed it at the man. "Who the fuck are you and what are you doing in my house?"

"I believe you knew my associate, Javier."

Before I could react, I was stabbed in the neck with something. I swung violently at whatever was behind me but hit the back of my hand into the wall. Whatever they injected me with was working fast. My vision became blurry and I was getting very light-headed.

I collapsed onto the floor, trying to keep myself awake. I reached into my pocket for my cell to call for help, but the man walked across the room and gently took it from my hands.

"Who the fuck are you?"

"Many call me the boss, but soon, you'll be calling me master."

To be continued...

About the Author

Andrew Hess, New York's King of Cliffhangers, found his love of writing while studying psychology at SUNY New Paltz. His debut book, Chamber of Souls (2011), depicted the life of a broken man wallowing in self pity. Using free verse poetry, he brought his character to life while journeying to find himself.

Hess picked up his first cliffhanger credit in 2013 with The Phoenix Blade Series (winner of Best Series Award in 2014 by Indie Author Books). The Phoenix Blade showcased a group of vigilante 20 year olds hired by the government to rid the country of the men and women who have evaded justice.

Hess continued his route down the path of mystery and suspense with the Detective Ryan Series, the Detective Thornton Series, and #1 Fan, which earned him the moniker King of Cliffhangers by several readers including the Fire & Ice Book Reviews.

Andrew won Indie Author Books: Best Mystery Thriller Author (2015), and Indie Author Books Series of the Year (2014) for The Phoenix Blade.

Andrew has been nominated for Best Male Author, Best Mystery Suspense Author, Book of the Year, and Best Mystery Book (2015) for Campus Killer.

By Wickedly Devine Divas, The Three Bookateers, & SNSBAH Promotions.

He was also nominated for Book of the year, and Best Mystery Book of 2015 for Campus Killer.

In 2016, he was nominated for the Summer Indie Awards in the Contemporary (#1 Fan), Crime (Conviction, and Deadly Games), Mystery (Campus Killer, Scorned, and Conviction), Romance (#1 Fan), and Anthology (Detours in Our Destinations).

Hess is also an avid blogger at The Writers Revolution (http://thewritersrevolution13.blogspot.com) and Between the Coverz (https://www.facebook.com/betweenthecoverz) where he promotes and interviews other authors, as well as reviewing books of all genres.

Stalking is not only acceptable but it's encouraged

FB
https://www.facebook.com/TheRealPhoenix13/

Twitter
https://www.twitter.com/Iamphoenix13

Amazon
http://www.amazon.com/Andrew-Hess/e/B00COCQJ5M/ref=sr_ntt_srch_lnk_1?qid=1462477104&sr=8-1

Trident Book Promotions FB
https://www.facebook.com/TridentBookPromotions/

Trident Book Promotions website
http://tridentbkpromotions.wix.com/tridentbookpromotion

Between the Coverz web
http://betweenthecoverz.wix.com/betweenthecoverz

Between the Coverz FB
https://www.facebook.com/betweenthecoverz/

Other Works by Andrew Hess

Poetry
Chamber of Souls
Hall of the Forgotten

The Phoenix Blade Series
The Phoenix Blade: Project Justice
The Phoenix Blade: Awakening
The Phoenix Blade: Pandemonium

Detective Ryan Series
Campus Killer (Detective Ryan Series Book 1)
Scorned (Detective Ryan Series Book 2)
Conviction (Detective Ryan Series Book 3)

Detective Thornton Series
Deadly Games (Detective Thornton Series Book 1)
Manhunt (Detective Thornton Series Book 2)

Strength Hope and Love Series
Finding Strength

Stand Alone Books
Trapped Inside: Living With Agoraphobia
Detours in Our Destinations
#1 Fan